U0126819

HOLD ON, LOVE!

**By Ching-Hsi Perng and Fang Chen
(Inspired by William Shakespeare's
AS YOU LIKE IT)**

English Translation by Ching-Hsi Perng

STUDENT BOOK CO., LTD.

HOLD ON, LOVE!
by Ching-Hsi Perng and Fang Chen
English Translation by Ching-Hsi Perng

Copyright © 2019 Ching-Hsi Perng and Fang Chen
                    cueariel@gmail.com
All rights reserved.
No.11, Lane 75, Sec. 1, He-Ping E. Rd., Taipei, Taiwan
http://www.studentbook.com.tw
email: student.book@msa.hinet.net

ISBN 978-957-15-1813-8

Translator's Note

Once again, it is with great pleasure and most sincere gratitude
that I record here my indebtedness to
two dear longtime friends:
Tom Sellari, Poet, Shakespearean scholar, and Professor
at National Chengchi University, Taiwan,
and
Joseph Graves, accomplished Actor, Director, Playwright,
and
Artistic Director of Peking University's
Institute of World Theatre and Film.
They read an earlier version of the translation
with loving care and critical acumen
and offered a wealth of useful suggestions for
improvement, especially regarding
the lyrics,
most of which have been incorporated here.
Any infelicities that remain are of course
solely my responsibility.

A Hakka adaptation of *Hold On, Love!*, premiered on 5 October 2019 at National Theatre, Taipei, Taiwan, was produced by Rom Shing Hakka Opera Troupe.

Original Script by Ching-Hsi PERNG and Fang CHEN
Hakka adaptation by Rom Shing Hakka Opera Troupe

Director	LE CHEN
Associate Director	CHUN-LANG HUANG
The King	KUO-CHING SU
Princess Xuelian (Xuelian)	YEN-LI CHIANG
Chamberlain Ji (Ji)	CHEN-YU HU
Director Mei (Mei)	YU-SHENG HU
Xinyan	CHIH-HOU CHEN
Mochou	DAI-CHEN WU
Tianheng	SZU-PENG CHEN
Hebo	BAI-YU DU
Doukou	TZU-YIN LIU
Quanjiao	YI-TING CHEN
Feiying	YI-JU CHEN
Composer	ROM-SHING CHENG
Costume Design	YU-FEN TSAI
Stage Design	MING-LUNG KAO
Light Design	WEN YUAN

Table of Contents

List of Characters

Lady Xin, Master Xin's wife

QUANJIAO   Actress of Xin Troupe; plays Li'l Tao and also
Lady Xin's maid servant

TANG   Director of Tang Troupe; plays A-de

FEIYING   Princess Xuelian's personal lady-in-waiting

SEVERAL LORDS

SEVERAL GUARDS

SEVERAL PALACE MAIDS

List of Scenes

Prelude

(Behind the gauze curtain upstage are vaguely seen lights and shadows of soldiers fighting. The Wuyou army, overpowering the Zixu troop, plants its standard on a mountain top.)

[Chorus, offstage]:
> **Bugles blasted, sabers clashed in moonlight,**
> **Till our brave cavalry carried the day.**
> **Attacks along the border changes made:**
> **No longer is Wuyou a vassal state.**
> **Upon deliberation Zixu's king**
> **His sister fair now offers to Wuyou.—**

(Stage light. Scene One begins.)

Scene 1: The Enquiry

(*Place: Wuyou's royal palace. The anteroom of* XUELIAN *'s bed chamber*)

XUELIAN: (*offstage, sings*)

>**Behind the mountains hang the floating clouds—**

(*slowly enters, sits, continues singing*)

>**In woods quite deep the sweet leaves of maple drift.**
>
>**My homeland vaguely in my dreams appears,**
>
>**And I, grief-stricken, for my mother cry.**
>
>**Romantic fancies of romantic youth**
>
>**Abruptly end with endless, streaking tears.**

(FEIYING *enters carrying a tea plate, places it on a side table, and stands in attendance.*)

>**By royal order a gift have I become.**
>
>**If only I were born a male instead!**

[Offstage, announcing]: Presents from His Majesty, the King!

(*Palace maids take turns showing* XUELIAN *diverse gifts.*)

MAID A: (*walking across the stage carrying a gold plate, sings*)

>**A pair of bracelets pearled, a necklace jeweled;**

XUELIAN: (*sings*)

>**I've always cared for only simple things.**

MAID B: (*walking across the stage carrying a silver plate, sings*)

> **Multicolored silk embroidered fine;**

XUELIAN: (*sings*)

> **My style is unadorned and plain attire.**

MAID C: (*walking across the stage with a jade plate, sings*)

> **A gorgeous fan with fancy tassels, oh;**

XUELIAN: (*sings*)

> **Can it compare with lasting poetry?**

MAID D: (*walking across the stage carrying a crystal plate, sings*)

> **A six-fold screen, a bottle made of jade.**

XUELIAN: (*sings*)

> **My boudoir is a reading room for me.**

(*Enter* JI, *who signals* MAID E *to bring in a hairpin box.*)

JI: (*ingratiatingly*) Your Highness, there is also this box of gold hairpins. . . .

XUELIAN: (*without even a look at it, waves her hand to the maid*) You are excused!

(*sings*)

> **While toward my native land I, sighing, look.**
> **My mission, dreadful, I must now fulfill.**

(JI *takes the hairpin box and signals* MAID E *to leave.*)

JI: (*profferring the box himself*) Your Highness, His Majesty—

XUELIAN: (*coldly*) You are also excused!

JI: Er . . .

[Offstage, announcing]: His Majesty, the King!

> (*Enter* THE KING, *greeted by* JI, *who gives a gesture of helplessness.* XUELIAN *arises and curtsies with* FEIYING.)
>
> (JI *steps aside.*)

THE KING: (*to* XUELIAN) Can Your Highness care for none of the gifts?

XUELIAN: Your Majesty, Wuyou had always submitted to Zixu, never neglecting the annual tribute. Now Your Majesty, who only recently ascended the throne, and who by surprise attack has won the battle, spreading fear throughout the land. The King, my brother, to calm our people, decided against a reckless, all-out war. Instead he sent me here to be your consort. Did I dare to disobey him? As to Your Majesty's bounteous presents, I don't really deserve them.—But I wonder how Your Majesty intends to deal with the defeated troop?

THE KING: Ah, how Your Highness' words embarrass us!—
(*sings*)

> **For years Wuyou and Zixu lived in peace;**
> **Like brothers we kept in frequent touch.**
> **But provocations led to confrontations.**
> **To guard our sovereignty, we did first strike.**
> **By Zixu peace has now been made with us;**
> **As equals, we'll have peace in both our lands.**

XUELIAN: (*kneels*) I thank Your Majesty.

THE KING: (*helps her up, sings*)

> **Our people welcome you, their future queen,**
>
> **And we Your Highness treat as honored guest.**
>
> **To win your smile these precious gifts we give:**

(*To* JI) Bring them here.

(JI *steps forward.* THE KING *takes the gold pins and sticks them gently into* XUELIAN*'s coil of hair.*)

(*sings*)

> **So to your charming movement swaying pins add charm.**

JI: (*with a flattering smile*) Won't they? See, they pale even the most gorgeous peonies in the royal garden!

XUELIAN: (*sings an aside*)

> **The royal favor is beyond compare,**
>
> **Still my heart's in my homeland far away.**
>
> **My distant country, my thought will keep close;**
>
> **I find no peace of mind at any price.**
>
> **To mend this mess it takes some cooling thought,**
>
> **Before connubial candle sears my heart.**

THE KING: My Lord Chamberlain. In ten days will come our nuptial hour. How goes preparations for the wedding?

JI: Everything's on schedule, Your Majesty. Nothing to worry about.

XUELIAN: (*suddenly interrupting*) Your Majesty, I am not well; my
head aches.

THE KING: (*concerned*) Is it the cold?

(*to* JI) Send for the royal doctor, quick!

JI: Yes, Your Majesty. (*about to leave*)

XUELIAN: (*stopping him*) That won't be necessary. All I need is
some rest. Please excuse me.

THE KING: Are you sure it's nothing serious?

XUELIAN: It's all right. Thank you, Your Majesty.

THE KING: Well . . . . Then take a good rest. We shall come and
visit you again soon.

(XUELIAN *bows, exits slowly.*)

THE KING: (*to Feiying*) Attend Her Highness well.

FEIYING: Yes, Your Majesty. (*Exit following* XUELIAN.)

THE KING: (*his eyes following* XUELIAN *as she exits*) My Lord
Chamberlain, have you been serving Her Highness well
since she arrived at the palace?

JI: We've followed Your Majesty's command with special
care: Forty-eight palace maids take turns serving Her
Highness without a second of slack.

THE KING: How about daily meals and necessities?

JI: Everything is furnished at our own elder princess' rate.

THE KING: Oh? Why, then, does Her Highness always seem so
depressed?

JI: Well . . . Perhaps too sudden Her Highness was commanded to travel from Zixu, in the far north, all the way to Wuyou for this unexpected marriage. Perhaps it's climate sickness, and she misses home.

THE KING: Oh? Is that so?

JI: Your Majesty, it is plain to all that you've treated Her Highness with the greatest possible respect. Just yesterday you ordered craftsmen to construct an annex in Zixu style. When that is completed, Her Highness will certainly be happy and not depressed.

THE KING: (*muttering*) It will be some time before the annex is completed. I need to find a way to please Her Highness now. . . .

JI: (*respectfully*) Yes. Your Majesty, your humble servant has learned that Her Highness the Princess loved theater while in Zixu and often befriended players. (*sounding out*) That Miss Xinyan of Mei Troupe is an excellent actress—shall we send for her to sing a couple of scenes to delight Her Highness?

THE KING: (*in deep thought*) Xinyan . . .

JI: (*perceiving something wrong, hastens to change the subject*) Or shall we call for a competition of our own Wuyou troupes, and let your humble servant select one among them to perform an exquisite comedy of love for the gala celebration ceremony. I guarantee that Her Highness, upon seeing the high artistic level of Wuyou, will certainly be wild with joy!

THE KING: Is this . . . feasible?

JI: Your Majesty—I have seldom said "I guarantee," but once I've guaranteed, has it ever proved otherwise?

THE KING: (*pauses a little*) Not that I know of.

JI: (*pointing to his head*) I dare guarantee with this my head, this plan will likewise not go wrong.

THE KING: (*hesitating*) Well, all right. Proceed with great care.

JI: Yes, Your Majesty. (*with undisguised pride*) It is my great honor to dispel my lord's worry. I'll go about it immediately. (*Exit.*)

THE KING: Xinyan . . . alas!

(*Light dims.*)

[Interlude]

(*A small lighted area on stage*)

(*Enter JI.*)

JI: His Majesty commands a propitious theater production. Now you all have passed my first-round selection and been awarded with a stipend. As long as you perform well, you will receive the second-round reward. His Majesty will appoint a top playwright to refine your script for production at the royal wedding ceremony. Moreover, you may be incorporated into the King's Troupe, to be stationed at the Royal Theater. So, go about it with diligence and care! (*Exit.*)

(*One by one, the directors of three theater troupes quickly enter and exit.*)

MEI: (*sings*)

> The upmost wants a play.
>
> The sun's about to set;
>
> So quickly I must work.
>
> Both food and drink forget!

TANG: (*sings*)

> The upmost wants a play,
>
> But I'm short-handed, see?
>
> A script is out of reach.
>
> An ant in a heated pot—that's me!

XIN: (*sings*)

> The upmost wants a play,
>
> Her Highness for to please.
>
> I'll innovate new rules:
>
> Remake's my expertise!

Scene 2: Rehearsing Love

(*Place: The rehearsal room*)

(*Players from the three troupes gather in the rehearsal room to warm up. They do splits, headstands, one-legged forward sways, somersaults, etc.*)

XIN: (*sings in rock'n'roll style Jingju*)

> Some are born great,
>
> Some achieve greatness,
>
> Some have greatness thrust upon them.
>
> Yet the greatest open their arms and bravely
> > embrace each other.

TANG: (*sings Kunqu*)

> Your beauty, though incomparable, cannot defy
> > time.
>
> Nowhere can I find you.
>
> In self-pity, you hide in the boudoir. . . .

(*Enter* MEI)

MEI: Hurry up! Hurry up! It's rehearsal time! The Lord Chamberlain is here already.

(XINYAN, *who plays Jiegeng, is dressed as a male in the disguise of Zhen Jishi;* MOCHOU, *who plays Linglan, is disguised as Zhen Jiqi, a country girl;* HEBO *plays Jester Ha. They start playing.* MEI *ushers* JI *to his seat. Exeunt the others.*)

XINYAN: (*sings*)

>**The princesses have masked themselves;**

MOCHOU: (*sings*)

>**Two sisters fled from court, to safety come.**

XINYAN: (*sings*)

>**Like flowing streams the time of life will pass;**

MOCHOU: (*sings*)

>**They must await their father king's return.**

HEBO: (*speaks*) Your Highnesses . . . .

MOCHOU: (*interrupting him*) Ha, you clown, you made a mistake again! My sister, now dressed as a man, is Master Zhen Jishih, owner of the farm, and I am Zhen Jiqi, a country maid. Now remember well.

HEBO: Yes, yes. My master and my lady. His Majesty the King, now on a state visit to Kitan, is not expected to return to the capital any time soon.

XINYAN: (*sings*)

>**Step-mother's craftiness we'll guard against;**

The faithful Nanny is our link at court.

(*speaks*) You, clown, come here. We will send a message to Nanny Jin in the court.—

(*murmurs something to* HEBO, *who keeps nodding his head*) Is that clear?

HEBO: Yes, sir.

(TIANHENG, *who plays Gu Liantian, enters with a traveling bag on his back.*)

XINYAN: Hush! Somebody's coming. Hide yourselves now.

(*Exeunt* MOCHOU *and* HEBO.)

TIANHENG: (*salutes with folded hands*) Er, young master, is this Forest Ali?

XINYAN: (*salutes with folded hands*) Yes. (*sizing up* TIANHENG; *aside*)

How like Brother Gu he looks . . . and yet, the way he dresses . . . ?

(*speaks*) My name is Zhen Jishi. What shall I call you, sir?

TIANHENG: This is Gu Liantian. Well met.

XINYAN: (*taken aback, speaks an aside*) So it *is* he!

(*trying hard to control herself*) Ah! Are you not the first-place winner of this year's national civil examination, son of the eminent Grand Counselor Gu. Yours is indeed a great noble family!

TIANHENG: You overpraise me, Master Zhen. You yourself speaks

in a most refined manner, unlike a country rustic. Did you
ever serve in the court and thus know my deceased father?

XINYAN: (*hurriedly*) No, no, no. All my life I've lived here. I
happen to have an uncle who is learned in the ways of the
world. With his instruction, I've come to know a thing or
two of the court.—What brings you here, may I ask?

TIANHENG: Well, I'm ashamed to tell you this—

(*sings*)

> **My father's corpse still's warm within the tomb,**
>
> **My elder, angry brother seeks my death!**
>
> **My great success on an exam**
>
> **Cannot protect me from his killing hand.**

(*speaks*) Were it not for my old servant, I would have been
in the nether-world by now, and not here.

XINYAN: Unbelievable! Why haven't you appealed to the King?

TIANHENG: His Majesty is out of the country, and nobody was in
charge. I can only keep myself hidden for the time being.

(*sings*)

> **Fate inexplicable makes a sport of me.**
>
> **This turmoil in me I cannot quell.**

(*speaks*) I heard that many plucky fellows are gathered in
this forest, under the leadership of Mo Baimen. He was a
good friend of my father's, so here I am to join him.

XINYAN: Master Gu—

(*sings*)

> All worldly glories are but shining dreams;
>
> For worldly fame tread men on ice so thin.
>
> Better to bask in nature's beauties through the
> year,
>
> And rise and fall with lilies of the field.

TIANHENG: (*sings*)

> In mountain life who'll keep you company?

XINYAN: (*sings*)

> The chirping birds and fragrant flowers speak.

TIANHENG: (*sings*)

> Can trees converse on shadows in the spring?

XINYAN: (*sings*)

> In serenity one sees through myriad things.

(*speaks*) Do not give up hope, Master Gu. Although you've lost a brother's love, at least you still have the loyalty of an old servant. Besides, Mo the band leader is a generous man of chivalry who upholds benevolence and righteousness. I'm sure you'll feel very much at home here.

TIANHENG: I thank you heartily for your comforting words, Master Zhen.

XINYAN: No need to be ceremonious among ourselves.

TIANHENG: Ourselves?

XINYAN: (*trying to cover up*) Er, yes, "Within the four seas all men are brothers," right? We are close friends. (*enthusiastically*) It's about two miles from here to Chief Mo's quarters. Allow me to be your guide.

TIANHENG: Much obliged.

(*Walking around the stage, they continue the performance in silence.*)

JI: Director Mei, what did you say this play is about?

MEI: (*with a pacifying smile*) My Lord, this play's called *Confusion upon Confusion*. After a series of coincidences and misunderstandings, the lovers are finally happily married.

JI: A bad title! It's taboo!

MEI: Ah?

JI: His Majesty the King is about to get married! How could there be any confusion? Not to say *Confusion upon Confusion*!

MEI: My lord, please instruct us then, for we need your guidance.

JI: Hmm—rename it *What Good Luck!*. It suits our Wuyou culture better.

MEI: (*fawningly*) Good, very good, my lord! Excellently renamed! That hits the nail on the head!

JI: (*proudly*) We can't be too careful about the celebratory performance! We need to read the mind of His Majesty!

MEI: Yes, yes, my lord, you're quite right . . . .

(XINYAN *walks out through the entrance door.*)

TIANHENG: (*retrieves a brush and turns to write a poem on a bamboo stalk*)

(*sings*)

> **In bamboo woods I write my lovelorn verse;**
> **A seed of love was planted years ago.**
> **Somewhere afar my dear one's wandering,**
> **Oh, when can reunited we twain be?**

(HEBO *enters, walking about aimlessly, and reads the verse.*)

> **To send my letter there, there's just no way:**
> **It's here the lovesick must his verse inscribe.**

HEBO: Ha! So an idiot has been painting on the bamboo!

TIANHENG: Wrong! It's a lovesick person writing his love poem.

HEBO: (*to the audience*) Lovesick person? Why, that's the same as an idiot, right? Love is merely a madness. Let's see what else have you written?

(*recites*)

> **Doubt thou the stars are fire;**
> **Doubt that the sun doth move;**
> **Doubt truth to be a liar;**
> **But never doubt I love.**

(*to* TIANHENG) Is this poetry? You composed it?

(*sarcastically*) Admirable talent!

TIANHENG: No. That one was by Prince Hamlet of Denmark. I just quoted him because I empathize with him. (*pointing to another bamboo*) That is my humble work.

HEBO: (*intones distortedly*)

> **All severance to desolation leads,**
>
> **And cloudy days . . .**

TIANHENG: (*interrupting him*) Not in this tone. Now listen—

(*sings*)

> **All severance to desolation leads,**
>
> **And cloudy days bring worries heavily.**
>
> **Let garish flowers show their beauty bold;**
>
> **I crave the quiet orchid in the dale.**
>
> **This rustic village has no tasty wine;**
>
> **The river cannot choose its time to bend.**
>
> **I've stood for long twixt heav'n and earth,**
>
> **Still there's no sight of her: just saddened eyes.**

HEBO: (*to the audience*) Aiyaa! What does all this mean?

(*to* TIANHENG) In my humble opinion, that verse by the Prince what's-his-name of Denmark is more moving. At least everybody can understand it. You, sir, please mar no more the bamboo woods—it's not eco-friendly.

TIANHENG: (*angry*) And you—pray you mar no more of my exquisite verses with your silly reading.

Ji: (*arise abruptly*) Stop! What's this you're performing? I guaranteed His Majesty the King he would enjoy an exquisite comedy of love!

Hebo: My Lord, it is said "This bud of love by summer's ripening breath may prove a beauteous flower when next the lovers meet." That is exactly what I've been acting: "Summer Breath Ripening the Bud of Love" . . .

(Mei *quickly lifts his hand to prevent* Hebo *from rambling on.*)

Mei: There's no need to worry, my lord! The exquisite part is coming up . . .

Ji: Hmm! How can I not worry? The nuptials are fast approaching, and you have rehearsed only one scene, and I don't know what this clown is doing.

Mei: Aiyaa, the quality of our performance is always guaranteed. As you know, of all the troupes in our whole country, only ours can boast of a complete cast. We may be a bit behind schedule, but with our professionalism, we can catch up quickly. Come back in two days, my lord, and I can guarantee a good show!

Ji: (*suspicious*) Don't you try to soft-soap me! This is no joking matter. The slightest misstep, and His Majesty will punish you home.

Mei: Rest assured, my lord. Your humble servant has always been dependable. It'll be fine, it'll be fine. . . .

JI: Hmm, the bamboo woods, (*offering advice*) here, here, and over there—there has to be some bamboo. See, there must be a couple of big rocks in this place, to make it look real. Also, get some Kungfu players to do some somersaults— that would be pretty. Key to a celebratory performance is liveliness, jollity. Understand?

MEI: Of course, of course. Your lordship is a true expert. What you said is perfectly right.

HEBO: (*to* TIANHENG) Alas, I'm afraid this will turn out a dud again.

TIANHENG: Sh—! Not so loud. (*with a wry smile*) Officials can't go wrong.

JI: I have something more to say.

MEI: Yes, sure, your lordship. I'm all ears.

JI: Where is Miss Xinyan?

MEI: Yes, sure. (*shouts to the stage entrance*) Xinyan—

(XINYAN *rushes in.*)

XINYAN: Did you call me, Director?

(MEI *winks to her.*)

(*turns to* JI) What is your command, my lord?

JI: Miss Xinyan, you ought to make a real good show. Although you've given many court performances, this time it is different. His Majesty the King, especially fond of

Princess Xuelian, takes this celebratory play very seriously. As the best actor of the country, you must double your efforts so that His Majesty won't lose face in front of the Princess.

XINYAN: Yes, my lord, I'll do my best.

JI: Hmm. Good, good.

(*to* MEI) It's getting late, and I must see the Xin Troupe now. Press on with your rehearsal.

MEI: Yes sir. Goodbye my lord, goodbye . . . . (*exit* JI, *accompanied by* MEI)

XINYAN: (*a multitude of feelings surging up; aside*) Little did I think—that His Majesty is *so* infatuated with the Princess . . . .

(*aside, sings*)

Bygones have faded like a puff of smoke;
It's clear that high and low can never match.
Just keep the longing of our love, and be
As pure as crystal ice in jadeite pot.

(*Light dims.*)

Scene 3: Genuine Feeling

(*Place: the Palace. The anteroom of the King's bedchamber*)

(THE KING *is conversing with* XUELIAN, *attended by* FEIYING.)

THE KING: (*with an embarrassed smile*) So it is for this that Your Highness has come at this late hour. The command performance for the festivity was meant to be a pleasant surprise for you. We didn't know the news has leaked out.

XUELIAN: (*smiles*) I thank Your Majesty for this kindness. (*pointing to* FEIYING) Feiyang happened upon the news and told me about it. (*pause*) I wonder if Your Majesty would allow me to oversee the selection of the play.

THE KING: Well—

XUELIAN: Your Majesty—

(*sings*)

> **The art of stage performance have I learned:**
> **"Four Basics and Five Rules" are hard indeed.**
> **But for the unexpected King's command,**
> **I'd still be watching plays in Zixu now.**

THE KING: (*sings*)

> **Well known's Your Highness' great intelligence,**

> Reputed expert in performing art.
>
> In Wuyou opera troupes are very few;
>
> Our players have a long, long way to go.

XUELIAN: (*sings*)

> There is no mirth in different customs here,
>
> And sitting idle in the court's such a bore.

THE KING: (*sings*)

> Imprudent actions give embarrassment;
>
> It always takes much time to purge the dross.

XUELIAN: (*sings*)

> A foreign land is ne'er as good as home—

THE KING: (*aside, speaks*) Ah, ne'er as good? Well, then—

(*speaks*) Your Highness may just—

(*sings*)

> Select the play, homesicknss to dispel.

XUELIAN: (*happy, speaks*) I thank Your Majesty!

Seeing how busy Your Majesty is, I'll withdraw.

(*She walks out of the door, where she drops her embroidered kerchief by accident. Exit with Feiying.*)

THE KING: (*muttering to himself*) Hard indeed it is to please this princess!

(*About to resume reading the memorials, he stops and goes to the corridor.*)

Alas, (*sings*)

The walls are high, the corridors are long,

(*Enter* XINYAN *in disguise, peeping and dodging from time to time.*)

XINYAN: (*sings*)

I've passed the wall, and circled corridors.

THE KING: (*sings*)

Beneath the moon, dark flower's trail I gaze,

XINYAN: (*sings*)

In moonlight dim, I weave on flower's trail.

THE KING: (*sings*)

At midnight does my longing stronger grow,

XINYAN: (*sings*)

At midnight do I slink and dash ahead.

THE KING: (*sings*)

The night is chilly and I'm all alone,

XINYAN: (*sings*)

The night is chilly but I'm unafraid.

(*hurriedly entering the palace, speaks*) Your Majesty!

THE KING: (*turning around, greets with joy*) Xinyan, I was just longing for you, and here you are!

XINYAN: (*grins*) Bless our telepathic minds!

THE KING: Alas—

(*sings*)

In bygone days, when but a bastard boy,

My only job was tending sheep in hills.

In bygone days, your sweet and merry laugh

Did comfort me, a poor and lowly worm.

(*both sinking into memory*)

THE KING: (*sings*)

By river's bank, was where we fell in love

With noble love and purity so true.

XINYAN: (*sings*)

White fish would then so suddenly appear.

Green shades, low branches, and the rolling clouds,

THE KING: (*sings*)

Light mist, fine rain, or under hazy moon,

We'd look for prince's feather in deep woods.

(*both returning to reality*)

THE KING: (*sings*)

How could we know the crown prince would die so

young,

And that the throne I therefore would ascend.

(*Enter Feiying, looking for the kerchief along the way.*)

FEIYING: Where could Her Highness' embroidered kerchief be?

(*arriving at the palace gate*) Ah, there it is!

(*She picks up the kerchief and, seeing* THE KING *holding*

XINYAN'*s hand, she hides herself and eavesdrops.*)

THE KING: (*sings*)

> In this small country, much we have to bear.
>
> The rule requires that I accept this match.
>
> To one I love, I broke my promise dear;
>
> In front of her I shamefully now stand.

XINYAN: (*speaks*) No, no, no. Your Majesty must not say so—

(*sings*)

> Enlightened monarchs put their countries first,
>
> And pay no heed to feelings of their own.
>
> My limits I will never overstep.
>
> The party o'er, to hometown I'll retire—

(*speaks*) In fact that's why I've come—to bid farewell to Your Majesty. I believe back home—

(*sings*)

> The willow trees are also fresh and green.

THE KING: (*cannot help but embrace* XINYAN) My Xinyan . . .

FEIYING: Oh my, which script is this? I'd better report to Her Highness. (*exit in a hurry*)

XINYAN: My lord—take good care of yourself!

(*Light dims.*)

[Interlude]

(*The King's Palace. The rehearsal room*)

(*Enter the* MEI *Troupe and the* XIN *Troupe with players in lively discussion; and then enter* TANG, *alone.*)

MEI: (*steps forward, sings*)

> **My super cast and all things else are ready.**

XIN: (*steps forward, sings*)

> **New lyrics, a new score, and a new style.**

TANG: (*seeing none behind, steps even more forward, sings*)

> **Survival instincts teach us how to cope.**

> (*Enter* JI.)

JI: (*sings*)

> **Her Highness, and not I, will choose the play.**

> (*speaks*) Now a different master must I serve!

[Offstage, announcing]: Her Highness the Princess!

JI: Now go get ready, you all.

ALL: Yes, my lord. (*exeunt*)

(*Scene Four starts.*)

Scene 4: Aspects of Love

(*Place:* THE KING*'s palace. The rehearsal room*)

(*Enter* XUELIAN, *attended by* FEIYING.)

XUELIAN: (*sings*)

> By king's decree I've come to choose the play;
>
> The premises I'll size up cautiously.
>
> It's serious: on it my fate depends.
>
> I must take care and not outsmart myself.
>
> The information I received last night
>
> Has changed my plan and I will nix this match.
>
> I tossed about last night for a fool-proof scheme;
>
> Propose one thing, another to achieve.
>
> Let's see how all these plays do now unfold.
>
> I'll watch—and find a way to lasting peace.

(JI *greets* XUELIAN. *She takes her seat.*)

JI: Your Highness, the theater competition of Wuyou's three top troupes will soon begin.

Here are the programs.

XUELIAN: Hmm.

(FEIYING *steps forward to accept them, shows them to*
XUELIAN, *who acknowledges with a mere glance.*)
(*The three troupes take turns to perform. The Tang Troupe
plays Kunju, the Xing Troupe plays rock 'n' roll Jingju [or
hip-hop Jingju, or musical Jingju], and the Mei Troupe
plays proper Jingju.*)

JI: Your Highness, the first show is *Midsummer Night's
Love.*—A fairy drops the charmed water on the wrong
person, so that when Ade wakes up, he falls in love with
Li'l Tao, totally forgetting Li'l Ya, who is eloping with
him. . . .

FEIYING: Your lordship needs not explain it. Her Highness is quite
familiar with the play.

JI: (*beating his own forehead*) Ah, how stupid I am! To have
forgotten that Your Highness is a connoisseur.

XUELIAN: (*smilingly*) Much obliged for your help.

JI: (*to stage entrance*) Commence the performance.

(*Enter* TANG *as Ade and* DOUKOU *as Li'l Ya on the
stage-on-the-stage.*)

DOUKOU: (*looking around*) But Director, there's nothing on the
stage!

TANG: Right, this is a minimalist theater.—The small budget

provided was only enough for costumes. The set must be imagined.

DOUKOU: Eh-oh. (*starts playing*) Ade, I betrayed my father to elope with you. How could you be so cruel as to desert me in this dark forest!

TANG: (*sings*)

> **Profound love calls, my fantasy runs wild.**

(*speaks*) As beauteous as the bright moon at night, Li'l Tao so enchants me. I'll just press on to meet her. Li'l Ya, our love affair is now over. Don't try to stop me.

DOUKOU: (*all sadness*) No, no, no! You are confused. This weird forest must have bewitched you so that you've forgotten your dearest love!

TANG: It's you who are confused. My love goes to Li'l Tao, forever and a day! Li'l Tao, Li'l Tao—here I come! (*exit*)

DOUKOU: No, Ade— (*exit, chasing Ade*)

(*Enter* QUANJIAO *as Li'l Tao and* TANG *from opposite directions.*)

TANG: Ah, is not that Li'l Tao? (*running up to her*) My dearest love!

QUANJIAO: (*startled*) Ade, are you mad? This is Li'l Tao, not Li'l Ya!

TANG: Please do not misunderstand. I have been in love with you for a long, long time.

(*sings*)

> **What brought about this amorous display?**
> **Most beautiful and charming of all blooms,**
> **My crazy longings pledge eternal love.**
> **This yearning will endure e'en after I am dead.**
> **Unending vows of love bear out my earnestness.**
> **Let time go by, but grant me marriage bed.**

QUANJIAO: Are you mocking me? You know full well that I can't get a sweet look from Master Mi, whom I love, and that has doomed me to everlasting perdition. Do I deserve further abuse like this? Deliver your speech to Li'l Ya!

TANG: (*hurriedly*) I'll pledge this: Never (*pointing to his heart*) is there anyone but you.

QUANJIAO: Here's a pledge, there's a pledge: they cancel each other out. How can I tell which is true?

TANG: I've said nothing but the truth. Why don't you, my dear, believe me?

QUANJIAO: Why must you mock me? Heavens! Do I deserve such mocking just because I've fallen in love with someone who doesn't love me?

(*sings*)

> **Tell me, Old Man Match-maker . . .**

(*Action continues in silence on the stage-on-the-stage.*)

XUELIAN: (*suddenly stirred, sings an aside*)

So love can go and grow this way or that;

To empty sadness such blind tangles lead.

Adhere to rules and you become a slave,

Adrift you go and toil for worthless things.

It's true small things may mirror something great.

Love is a word worth much considering.

(*curtain call on the stage-on-the-stage*)

JI: (*begging instructions*) What does Your Highness think of this
play?

XUELIAN: (*back to her senses*) They did well. Go and receive the
reward.

(JI *waves his hand.*)

TANG AND QUANJIAO: I thank Your Highness.

(*Exit* QUANJIAO.)

TANG: (*wiping off sweat, speaks an aside*) Mine is a one-man troupe,
looks good outside, but empty inside. I courted the special
favor of Doukou and Quanjiao of the Xin Troupe, to guest
perform in this show and have escaped unscathed. What
sheer luck! (*exit*)

FEIYING: What is the next troupe's play about?

JI: Your Highness, the next play is *Madame Xin, the Chaste*,
performed by the Xin Troupe.—I heard it's a rock'n'roll
Jingju. Because they changed the script at the last moment,
I haven't seen it. Director Xin stresses that it is a good play

that sings the praise of virtuous women. We look forward
to your evaluation.

FEIYING: A "rock'n'roll Jingju"?

XUELIAN: That's something new indeed.

JI: (*to the stage entrance*) Commence the performance.

> (*Enter stage hands with a table and two chairs.*)
>
> (*Enter* DOUKOU *as Madam Xin, who takes the host's seat
> and reads a letter. She is accompanied by* QUANJIAO *as a
> maid servant.*)
>
> (*Enter* XIN *as Hu Bao.*)

XIN: (*sings*)

> **I am a playboy, my name is Hu Bao.**
>
> **Well known throughout the capital I am.**
>
> **Who doesn't know, or who's unaware**
>
> **That every night on brothel girls I call.**
>
> **The other day one Master Xin arrived.**
>
> **He bragged about the beauty of his wife,**
>
> **And wagered on her truth an egg-sized pearl.**
>
> **To Wujiang therefore I have come.**

(*speaks*) So it was that in a wine shop I chanced upon one
Master Xin, a merchant from Wujiang. After a few cups of
wine, he made this bet: if I could not seduce his virtuous
wife, I'd lose a pearl that shines at night. So, (*taking the
guest seat*) to make a long story short, I've come to his

home to deliver his letter.

DOUKOU: (*folds the letter*) Master Hu, how does my husband in the capital, Bianliang?

XIN: (*prevaricating*) Er . . . well . . .

DOUKOU: (*puzzled*) What's so difficult, Master Hu? Please tell me the truth and hide nothing.

XIN: Ah, I feel so sorry for you, ma'am.

DOUKOU: Oh? What does this mean?

XIN: Normally I wouldn't gossip behind my friend's back, but he—

(*sings*)

> **In house of mirth with singing girls he stays,**
> **Each night he wines and dines until he's soused.**
> **Close female friends he keeps where'er he goes:**
> **In Wujiang he is quite notorious.**

DOUKOU: Is my husband so dissolute?

XIN: Isn't he? I feel truly sorry for you, excellent lady—if only I could be admitted to your intimate presence, stroke your slender hand so smooth, and kiss your pretty cheek, I'd never be like that unappreciative Master Xin, who throws away his own gem to look for cheap glass elsewhere. . . .

DOUKOU: What language is this? This is despicable! Get out of here! I can't take it anymore. . . .

JI: (*sharply*) Hold it! *I* can't take it anymore!

(*Frightened,* XIN, DOUKOU, *and* QUANJIAO *stop playing.*)

(*to* XUELIAN) I don't know what this chaotic mess is about! What a shame to the God of Drama! Please forgive us, Your Highness. I will surely punish the Xin Troupe hard.

XUELIAN: (*to* XIN) What is all this?

XIN: (*feeling injured*) Your Highness, we planned to perform *What You Will,* but the Lord Chamberlain said it is ominous . . .

QUANJIAO: (*cutting in*) It's a comedy in which Ms. Weiaola desperately longs for King Yili, and finally the two get married. . . .

XUELIAN: Oh—? (*turning to* FEIYING, *in low voice*) Is this the one?

FEIYING: (*in low voice*) No, it's Xinyan of the Mei Troupe.

XIN: (*stopping* QUANJIAO) Nonsense. Anyway, Lord Ji requested that we change the play, and I thought, *Madame Xin, the Chaste* is not bad—No matter how Hu Bao seduces her, she holds fast to proper conduct and remains chaste. . . .

JI: So you're arguing? How dare you?

XIN: My lord, I have spoken nothing but the truth. I dare not deceive you, my lord. In order to put on this new play, the entire troupe worked day and night, around the clock, without a moment's rest.

QUANJIAO: (*aside*) Right. He violated the Labor Standard Law.

DOUKOU: (*stopping her*) Don't you pour oil on the fire!

XUELIAN: (*to* FEIYING) It seems that this play reflects the sad
condition of women, who are born enthralled. Once
married, they may seem mistresses of the house, but are in
fact still accessories.

FEIYING: Exchangeable with a pearl. Easily swapped. Pitiable
indeed. Madame Xin, a mere puppet!

JI: (*aside*) Well—how shall I reply? Could Her Highness the
Princess . . .

(*to* XUELIAN) These coarse jokes of the Xin Troupe are too
much. Let me just dismiss them. . . .

XUELIAN: Chamberlain Ji, I'll see to it.

JI: Yes, Your Highness.

XUELIAN: (*to* XIN, DOUKOU, *and* QUANJIAO) You are excused
for now.

XIN, DOUKOU, AND QUANJIAO: We thank Your Highness.

(*Exeunt.*)

FEIYING: (*to* XUELIAN) It looks like we can't have high
expectation for the celebratory play.

JI: (*embarrassed*) Your Highness, we do have some relatively better
organized troupes, such as this last one. With adequate
personnel for administration, acting, and production, they
may well be called Wuyou's number one troupe.

XUELIAN: Oh? What is their play?

JI: *What Good Luck!—*

(FEIYING *bursts into laughter;* XUELIAN *signals no to her.*)

(*hurriedly*) It's original title was *Confusion upon Confusion.* The new title was my idea.

XUELIAN: Undoubtedly for its auspicious implication? Very thoughtful of you.

JI: (*proudly*) Yes, indeed. The Mei Troupe will be performing a regular Jingju. The play tells of two princesses who are persecuted by the queen their step-mother while the king is away on a state visit. So they run away in a hurry with the court jester to Forest Ali. For convenience's sake, Jiegeng, the elder sister, dresses as a male and becomes the owner of a farm house. By coincidence, her childhood play mate Gu Liantien, the first-place winner of the civil examination, also seeks shelter in the forest. And the two meet . . . .

(XUELIAN *and* FEIYING *look at each other, then* XUELIAN *motions to* JI.)

Commence the performance.

(*Enter* TIANHENG *as Gu Liantian. He writes verses on bamboo. Enter* XINYAN *as Jiegeng, dressed as Zhen Jishi.*)

XINYAN: (*smiling, surveying the bamboos*) You're in high spirits, my brother!

TIANHENG: You laugh at me. But even though life in the wild is difficult, it cannot change my true love.

XINYAN: Why are you writing verses on all these bamboos, sir?

TIANHENG: Alas, to be honest with you, I am a very unhappy man.

XINYAN: (*concerned*) Oh? How so?

TIANHENG: Oh brother mine—

> (*sings*)
>
> **Don't blame me if distracted now I seem;**
>
> **A thirsting of one's heart is hard to quench.**
>
> **The years wear on but news there's none. To this**
>
> **Bamboo alone can I express my love.**

XINYAN: (*shocked, sings an aside*)

> **When we were small, we'd often run and play**
>
> **In palace garden side by side, or seek**
>
> **Daylilies to make us worry-free.**
>
> **Now reunited, friends we have become.**

(*Recalling their innocent childhood, she sobs, but quickly conceals her true feelings.*)

> **Old Man under the moon, the match-maker,**
>
> **Can you unfeeling watch us split in two?**

XUELIAN: (*aside, sings*)

> **As clear-bright as the moon she's shown her mind.**
>
> **Her love sea-deep she never can discard.**

XINYAN: (*aside*) I'll get to the bottom of this.

XUELIAN: (*aside*) I'll have this clarified.

XINYAN: (*speaks*) May I ask you, my brother, who is the one you love?

TIANHENG: Er . . . If I tell you, you must promise to keep the secret.

XINYAN: By heaven, I'll never reveal even one syllable of it.

TIANHENG: It's two syllables.

XINYAN: Which two syllables?

TIANHENG: (*in low voice*) Jie—geng—

XINYAN: (*dumbfounded*) What?

TIANHENG: Her Highness the Princess—

XINYAN: (*shocked, suspecting her identity exposed*) Ah—

TIANHENG: (*sings*)

> The princess and I: together we grew up as bosom
> friends,
> Three full years, full three years, happy study-
> mates were we.

XINYAN: (*remembering* THE KING, *sings an aside*)

> The princess and he: their nuptials are made public
> to the world.
> Celebratory play, a play to celebrate: true or false
> the wedding candles burn.

TIANHENG: (*sings*)

> For the princess,
> Every morning I walked around the palace
> walls,
> And watched into the night till mid-night

struck.

XINYAN: (*sings an aside*)

> **For the princess,**
>
> **He thinks he needs to build an annex,**
>
> **Forgetting all about our friendship old.**

TIANHENG: (*sings*)

> **As first-place winner of civil exam,**
>
> **I thought she'd be my happy bride.**

XINYAN: (*sings an aside*)

> **To roam about the wide world long,**
>
> **I thought he'd be my happy mate.**

TIANHENG & XINYAN: (*together, sing*)

> **Alas! I'm stuck in wilderness so wild,**
>
> **And where's the cure for my disease of love?**

(*As* XINYAN *is lost in sadness,* TIANHENG *has to remind her.*)

TIANHENG: (*repeating himself, sings*)

> **—the cure for my disease of love?**

XINYAN: (*back to her senses, pretending to be pleasantly surprised, sings an aside*)

> **A song so sad my brother sang,**
>
> **He's laid his cards all on the table.**

(*About to reveal herself, she changes her mind and speaks an aside.*)

Hold on!—

(*sings an aside*)

"A hasty move alarms the bird."

I'll—wait until my grievance is redressed.

(*speaks*) A truthful love indeed, my brother. How fortunate
this princess! How I envy her!

TIANHENG: (*smiles bitterly*) What's there to envy? The princess is
totally ignorant of this. Besides, after years of separation,
we may not know each other even when we meet.

(XINYAN *chuckles.*)

In this one-sided-love affair I am director and actor. How
miserable!

XINYAN: (*relieved*) My brother, you must not be so hard on yourself.
True love is hard to come by nowadays. You command my
respect. (*pondering*) Well, then, let me find a good remedy
to cure you of this love-sickness.

TIANHENG: What good remedy? Can it really dispel my grief?

XINYAN: No problem. Let me play the princess.

TIANHENG: Ah?

(XINYAN *goes on to explain to* TIANHENG. *There are
movements, but no sound.*)

XUELIAN: (*as if enlightened, speaks an aside*) "Play the princess"?
"A good remedy" . . .

(*sings an aside*)

> **There's tons of water in the wide, wet world,**
>
> **But only single cup will I imbibe.**
>
> **If your companion's not a fitting mate,**
>
> **To part will lead you on a better way.**

(*aside*) This union arranged by my brother-king is in fact a forced marriage, in which there is no joy at all. Why don't I seek a new way, by means of a play? Perhaps there will be a slight chance? Besides, this girl Xinyan . . .

(*sings an aside*)

> **Entrusted with the pow'r to choose the play,**
>
> **I'll write the plot anew for the good king.**
>
> **A twist so sly may change the world, they say.**
>
> **The celebration I'll use to tell the truth.**
>
> **New play shall lead to situations new.**
>
> **The ending of the drama must be changed.**
>
> **Director of my script is what I'll be—**
>
> **Compared with gain, the hardship hardly hurts!**

(*her mind made up, she arises and speaks*) Well, let's call it a day here.

(TIANHENG *and* XINYAN *freeze.*)

JI: But Your Highness, the play is not finished yet! This drama competition . . .

(MEI *rushes up.*)

XUELIAN: Well?

JI: Ah, this is Director Mei. (*to* MEI) You are too rude . . .

MEI: Please forgive me, Your Highness and Your Lordship. The desperate situation made me forget my manners. You see, the best part of our rehearsal comes next. Your Highness, I . . .

XUELIAN: (*smilingly, to* MEI) Don't worry.

         (*to* JI) Your Lordship was right. The Mei Troupe has the best players. Their performance is lively and their movement nimble. Quite expressive and moving. They deserve to be called of the best troupe of Wuyou. The Mei Troupe shall perform the celebratory play.

JI: Your Highness judges well.

MEI: I thank Your Highness! I thank Your Highness!

XUELIAN: We are not finished yet.

MEI: Please give your order, Your Highness. I'm all ears.

XUELIAN: (*deliberately*) Suppose we want to revise some of the arias and speeches, add or delete certain plot points—would that be all right?

JI: (*surprised*) Er . . .

MEI: No problem, no problem. No problem of course. It would be our great honor to receive Your Highness' favor and instruction. Your humble servants will do their best.

XUELIAN: Very well. Come back tomorrow, for we will give you some instructions.

MEI: Yes, sure. I thank Your Highness.

XUELIAN: Let's go.

(*Exeunt* XUELIAN, FEIYING, *and* JI.)

MEI: God speed Your Highness!

(*The actors bow.*)

(*waves to* TIANHENG *and* XINYAN. TIANHENG *steps forward*) Tomorrow when we go to the palace, you two . . .

(*Exeunt with* TIANHENG, *conversing.*)

XINYAN: (*aside*) I wonder what Her Highness has in mind. Ai—

(*sings an aside*)

> **One half of this is life, and half but theater;**
>
> **Half concealed, half self-deception.**
>
> **What if I can't my feelings true quite hide,**
>
> **And on the carpet red my love reveal?**

(*Light dims.*)

Intermission

Scene 5: Love Awakened

(*Place: The Palace. The rehearsal room*)

(*The Mei Troupe is rehearsing. Enter* MOCHOU *as Linglan, dressed as Zhen Jiqi.*)

MOCHOU: (*looking around aimlessly, sings*)

> Is it reality or fantasy—
> One turn around, I'm in another world:
> Green mountain visible 'neath the melon shed,
> Farm houses dot the old crisscrossing paths.
> The plain is not a plain from paintings old,
> But touched up here and there with flora wild.

(*looks at a bamboo, sings on*)

> "My love in this sad dream I dream in vain;
> "Deep in the woods is heard the croaking frog."

(*counting with her fingers, speaks movingly*) This is the forty-ninth bamboo!

(*Enter* HEBO *as Youha the clown.*)

HEBO: My dear lady, so you've strolled here. The master sends for you.

MOCHOU: (*excitedly*) Did you see, Youha? These inscribed

verses—what profound love!

(*intones*) "Poor yellow flowers, buried in dirt, / Dying, they dare not loudly wail"; "I meditate: old love's a thing of the past, / West winds have only sadness brought". . . How very touching!

HEBO: My dear lady, the truest love poems are the most exaggerated. The pledges in them are mostly feigned—they don't have to be fulfilled.

MOCHOU: What an absolute blockhead you are!

HEBO: Alas, fools may not speak wisely while wise men do foolishly.

MOCHOU: Enough of this nonsense! Hey, do you know who wrote these?

HEBO: The writer of these verses, he is awfully sick!

MOCHOU: What do you mean?

HEBO: He is that Master Gu. It is said that he is so love-sick, he has to come to our farm often to . . .

MOCHOU: (*interrupts*) Doesn't he come to improve his learning through discussion with my sister?

HEBO: Love-sickness is a kind of learning worthy of serious study.

MOCHOU: (*pauses, coming to realize*) Could it be that my sister . . .

(*Enter* XUELIAN, FEIYING, *and* MEI *with a script.*)

XUELIAN: (*interrupting* MOCHOU, *to* MEI) We shall revise from here! What do you think, Director Mei?

MEI: (*looking at the script, respectfully*) Yes, yes, yes. Your humble servant will start rehearsing this minute.

(*beckons* MOCHOU *and* HEBO, *gives them their parts, gesturing*) The two of you . . . thus . . . thus . . . .

Understand?

(MOCHOU *and* HEBO *keeps nodding.*)

(*Enter* XINYAN *as Jiegeng, cross-dressed as Zhen Jishi.* MEI *walks to her and gives her her part.*)

XINYAN: So this is—?

MEI: This is it. From here on, we'll follow Her Highness' revised version!

XINYAN: (*leafing through the script, muttering to herself*) In this new version—I seem to be playing . . . a different princess . . .

MEI: (*to* MOCHOU *and* HEBO) Come here, you start from "Love-sickness is . . ." again.

HEBO: (*looking at the script*) Love-sickness is a kind of learning worthy of serious study.

MOCHOU: (*looks at the script, pauses, suddenly realizing*) No wonder he always seems heavy-hearted. Could it be that I have . . . (*laughs*) Youha, let's go back now. (*exit running*)

HEBO: What's the hurry, my lady? Wait for me, my lady! (*exit, running after her*)

XUELIAN: (*to* MEI) Go on with the rehearsal. We have written new arias for Princess Jiegeng. . . .

(*Enter* MOCHOU *with the script.* MEI *walks to her, and the two discuss the play on Upstage Right.*)

XINYAN: (*glances at the script, sings*)

> **Some trips to mountain tops, and spring is gone,**
>
> **An easy life I've led like fairy dream.**
>
> **I seem to have forgotten time at court;**
>
> **Without my knowing, settled in the woods.**
>
> **Disguised, I suffer pains that no one knows.**
>
> **Like wind, I fear, away goes fleeting time.**
>
> **To whom can I reveal my feelings deep?**
>
> **Alone at midnight, facing a lonely lamp. . . .**

XUELIAN: (*to* XINYAN) Here you should show an unnamable gloomy mood, with intense feeling. You lack empathy.

XINYAN: (*resumes singing*)

> **The blooms, no rival of the jealous wind and rain,**
>
> **All fall aground, or drift to arid land along the stream.**

XUELIAN: (*to* XINYAN) This won't do. There's no genuine feeling. Make it more subtle!

XINYAN: (*patiently*) Yes. (*takes a few glances at the script, then starts*) Alas, it's been several months since I disguised myself and came to this forest. Although Master Gu pays me daily visit, which helps dispel my sorrow, yet this disguise causes much inconvenience. I wonder what's going on in the court, and whether the king my father has returned to the palace. How I miss him!

XUELIAN: It's Princess Linglan's cue!

(*Enter* MOCHOU *hurriedly.* XUELIAN *talks with* MEI *in a low voice, frequently gesturing.*)

MOCHOU: (*glancing at the script from time to time*) Sister, sister, what do you think of Master Gu?

XINYAN: Why ask about him all of a sudden?

MOCHOU: Never mind why, just tell me. Do you think he—

XINYAN: Brother Gu—

(*sings*)

> **Why Brother Gu—**
>> **He's dashing eyebrows, starry eyes, and**
>> **brilliant mind;**
>> **He's moral, noble, a man of integrity.**
> **Oh, Brother Gu—**
>> **His comments always clear and reasoned well:**
>> **A rare, outstanding person in this world.**

MOCHOU: (*sings*)

>> **It is well known he loves a special one;**
>> **He gladly takes the time to visit us.**
>> **How deeply lovelorn is this man? Who in**
>> **The bamboo woods his secret sorrow writes.**

XINYAN: (*sings an aside*)

> **In secret have I pledged my heart in love,**

XUELIAN: (*interrupts, to Xinyan*) Your feeling has drifted away.

> Have you not pledged your heart in love?

XINYAN: (*aside*) Ah, why does Her Highness keep finding fault with me?

MOCHOU: (*sings on*)

> **I hope my royal father comes back soon.**

XINYAN: (*sings*)

> **The sky will clear when all the rain is done,**

MOCHOU: (*carried away, sings*)

> **I'll ever be with Master Gu: What joy!**

XINYAN: (*shocked*) What? You . . .

MOCHOU: Dear sister, to be honest, I've long admired brother Gu. . . . (*bashful*) When we get back to the palace, would you, dear sister, help me persuade our royal father?

XINYAN: (*apprehensively*) Persuade him to do what?

> (*Enter* HEBO *in a rush.*)

HEBO: One minute's delay, and the princess will be making stairs to marriage.

XINYAN: "Stairs to marriage"?

HEBO: That is, "offering presents," "enquiring after the name and horoscope," "informing the result," "tendering cash gifts," "proposing an auspicious date," and "escorting the bride"—

the entire ceremonial process leading to matrimony. Thus, step by step, they climb higher and higher, and finally enter the nuptial chamber.

XINYAN: Ah, this . . .

MOCHOU: (*bashful*) Aiya! (*like a spoiled child*) Sister, oh my dear sister!

(*Cooing of a pigeon is heard.*)

HEBO: (*looking up*) Oh, it must be Nanny Jin's message.

MOCHOU: Dear Sister!

XINYAN: Alas!—

(*sings an aside*)

> **Incessant sighs for unexpected things;**
> **Nature's twists turn maple trees to locust.**
> **My sister can't abide festoons for weddings,**
> **Awakening of love now dawns on her.**
> **She longs to deck her hair with pretty flow'rs,**
> **She sows adoring seeds within her heart.**

MOCHOU: (*entreating*) My sister! My dear sister!

XINYAN: (*sings*)

> **Her ceaseless, girlish voice now hits my ear.**
> **Her bosom is imbued with tears—so sad!**

(*sighs, speaks*) Ah, my dear sister—

(*sings*)

> **Matrimony is a solemn thing.**

I must think twice before I decide.

XUELIAN: (*interrupts, to* XINYAN) That's right! "Matrimony is a solemn thing." Remember that well!

XINYAN: Yes. (*aside*) Is Her Highness suggesting something?

MOCHOU: (*happy, sings*)

> **With scarlet silk I'll tie the lover's knot;**
>
> **My sister I'll entrust with tailoring.**

(XINYAN *lightly pats* MOCHOU.)

(*Enter* HEBO *hurriedly with a small piece of paper.*)

HEBO: Good news!—After His Majesty the King's return to the court, Nanny Jin found occasion to give a detailed report. Learning the truth after investigation, His Majesty put the queen under house arrest, and dispatched imperial guards to escort Your Highnesses back. Now we may pack and get ready to return to the palace.

XINYAN: Ah, thank heavens!

MOCHOU: (*clapping her hands*) How wonderful! We're returning to the palace!

HEBO: But—

XINYAN: What else did Nanny say?

HEBO: His Majesty has struck a nuptial agreement with the Khan . . . .

XINYAN & MOCHOU: (*alarmed*) What?

HEBO: According to Nanny Jin, to secure peace along the borders,

His Majesty has decided to form an alliance between the two countries. Hence the nuptial league.

XINYAN: Ah!

(XINYAN *almost faints, but* MOCHOU *quickly steadies her with her hands.*)

MOCHOU: Sister! What's to be done now?

XINYAN: Alas—

(*with genuine feeling, sings an aside*)

> How I wish—in spring, with flow'rs abloom,
> I'd paint my face in colors of rich bliss.
> Likeminded unions, how I wish they'd last.
> Let love be constant and endure like rock.
> Who would have known—such storms come from
>   blue sky!
> The earth does quake, and heavens shatter too.
> A sudden blizzard withers all the plants.
> Into the wilderness old love is tossed!

XUELIAN: (*aside*) Just as I suspected, there's none but the King in her mind.

XINYAN: (*sings*)

> On sister's fancy I must counsel her,
> On father's will I cannot contradict.
> My feeling's mixed, my thoughts awhirl, confused:
> Like weeds on water, so I drift along.

XUELIAN: (*cuts in, to* XINYAN) Very good! Act like this in the celebratory performance. Especially crucial is the last part. Pay extra attention to it.

XINYAN: (*glances at the script, shocked*) But—the Princess actually . . .

XUELIAN: (*interrupting*) Exactly. In life one must have ideas of one's own, and be brave enough to pursue one's goal. A compromised life is—(*pointing to the script*) not worth living. (*to* XINYAN, *in a slow, deliberate voice*) Do you understand?

XINYAN: (*her feelings mixed*) Yes, your servant understands.

XUELIAN: Good. (*to all*) For we must remember—

(*sings*)

> **Like dreams our lives we act out on the stage.**
> **Each hue and shape theatrically appears.**
> **The base and low its ugliness can't hide,**
> **While beauty shines and virtues are upheld.**
> **From scene to scene, our play unfolds the world.**
> **An actor's words, for sure, are worth a lot.**
> **They are not illusions, plays are tangible,**
> **Revealing stuff of story, old and new.**
> **If you can play with heart and diligence,**
> **You will be able to enlighten all.**

(*speaks*) You must work hard the next few days to polish

your acting, so that the performance can resemble real life.

ALL: Your Highness may rest assured that we will do our utmost best.

XUELIAN: (*to* MEI, *pointing to the script*) Rehearse this section again. The princess should . . .

(*She discusses it with* MEI *in a low voice.*)

XINYAN: (*muttering to herself*) I enact the princess' life. What about my own?

MOCHOU: What's on your mind?

XINYAN: Well, I was just thinking—if the princess can rewrite her life, can we all do the same with ours?

HEBO: Of course. (*to the audience*) Haven't we already done it?

(*Light dims.*)

Scene 6: Love Remembered

(*Place: The Grand Hall of the Wuyou Palace*)

(*Music. Enter* GUARDS, MAIDS, LORDS, FEIYING, *and* JI, *each taking their places.*)

[Chorus, offstage]:

> **The king's procession dazzles as it gleams**
> **With jewelry bright. Dewdrops give off scent,**
> **The palace is ablaze with blazing plants,**
> **And tiles glazed green, and banisters bright red!**
> **From eaves, the dangling wind chimes music make,**
> **While lion-shaped golden censer all night burns.**

(MEI *rushes onto the stage and clings to* JI.)

MEI: My lord, my lord . . .

JI: What's the matter? Why this pell-mell dash?

MEI: Yesterday Hebo, who plays Youha the clown, stumbled on the set backstage and fell down the staircase. His leg is broken . . .

JI: (*furious*) How could you, Director Mei! How is the show to go on now?

[Offstage, announcing]: His Majesty the King and Her Highness the

Princess!

JI: You—you . . . it's none of my business if you wish to have your head chopped off, but why have you gotten me into this mess?

MEI: It's all right now, my lord. Even last night I begged Director Xin to play the clown's part.

JI: Hmm! At least you're smart. Now get lost!

MEI: Excuse me. (*exit*)

(THE KING *and* XUELIAN *take their seats.*)

[Chorus, offstage]:

> **With grace the king so many gifts presents:**
>
> **That's how male phoenix woos the female's love.**

JI: My Lord, Troupe of Mei . . . er . . . and Troupe of Xin jointly present—

(*looks at the program, surprised*) *Confusion . . . upon . . . Confusion* to celebrate the royal marriage.

THE KING: Good!

JI: Commence!

(*Lighting on the performing area. Enter* MEI.)

MEI: Here's the plot summary of the first part of *Confusion upon Confusion* with gongs and drums. (*exit*)

(*After a segment of gongs and drums, enter* XINYAN *as Jiegeng dressed as Master Zhen Jishi, and* TIENHENG *as Gu Liantian. They walk around a little, and then face each other.*)

TIANHENG: My dear brother, you sent for me with such urgency. What's the serious business?

XINYAN: Dear brother mine, to tell you the truth: I am—Jiegeng herself.

TIANHENG: Ah! you are Princess Jiegeng?

XINYAN: Even she.

TIANHENG: (*looking at her up and down, pleasantly surprised*) My dear brother—no, Your Highness, how you've fooled me all this time!

XINYAN: Ah, dear brother—

(*sings*)

> I didn't mean to hide the fact from you,
> But I must guard against the evil queen.
> My royal father's back home now, and all
> Dark clouds removed, the sun shines once again.

TIANHENG: (*sings*)

> For you Your Highness how I've sighed!
> Adversity at home has tortured me.
> Dear brother, your companionship has made
> This forest life a peaceful one for me.
> But now, you suddenly the princess turn,
> And parting's sorrow e'en the willows know!

XINYAN: My dear brother is mistaken—

(*sings*)

> I bid farewell to you, to court return,
>
> But will return with marriage order soon.

TIANHENG: (*overjoyed, sings*)

> When spring breeze brushes willows by the bank,
>
> When butterflies and bees make honey sweet,
>
> It's not too late for us to be as one:
>
> Gu Liantian is bliss, now bad luck's gone!

XINYAN: (*sings*)

> My younger sister is so fond of you
>
> That she will be your happy bride.

TIANHENG: (*shocked*) What? Your younger sister—Princess Linglan?

XINYAN: Yes. Linglan has a crush on you, my brother. Your marriage will surely be most happy and harmonious.

TIANHENG: Well, er, I don't know where to start . . . . Then, then— how about you?

XINYAN: Ah, my dear brother—

(*sings*)

> It's ordered that I marry Kitan's chief
>
> To form a league and try to keep the peace.
>
> When party's over, guests disperse, go home.
>
> Your favor I will always bear in mind.
>
> Alas, the luck of lover's just not ours;

> Let's cultivate it in another world.

TIANHENG: No, no—

> (*sings*)
>
> > These words have all the world so murky made,
> >
> > As if my heart is shot through by thousand darts!
> >
> > Small waters don't impress when you've seen seas.
> >
> > When deeply hurt, one is even numb to cold.
> >
> > I now refuse to be king's son-in-law.
> >
> > My love profound, I have no word to God.

XINYAN: My brother, please don't say so.

TIANHENG: No! All my life, you'll be my only love!

> (*sings*)
>
> > My share of this life's happiness falls short,
> >
> > I'm resolved to be a monk, to cultivate some better
> >
> > > luck .

> (*Exit resolutely.*)

XUELIAN: (*to* THE KING) In love, one must follow one's heart.

> Doesn't Your Majesty agree?

THE KING: Well . . .

> (*sings*)
>
> > His eyes are only set on one, I see.
> >
> > But now the two are forced to part, and oh,
> >
> > How hard this separation surely is!
> >
> > Can boat no ripples make where it floats by?

(*Enter* XIN *as Youha.*)

XIN: Your Highness, why torment yourself in this way?

XINYAN: Fool, you don't understand.

XIN: What's so hard to understand? Master Gu loves you profoundly, yet contrarily you insist on matching him with Princess Linglan. There is no misery worse than marrying someone you don't love!

(XINYAN *sobs, as does* XUELIAN.)

THE KING: (*touched, sings an aside*)

> My loved one, face half covered, softly weeps:
> A beautiful pear blossom in the rain.

(*to* XINYAN)

> Could it be that you act against your will?

(*to* XUELIAN)

> Could it be that you miss your homeland far?
> Or could it be that parties drain your strength?

(*pauses, then resumes singing*)

> Or maybe there's much more than meets the eye?

XUELIAN: (*to* THE KING, *sings*)

> Some truth there is in this true play. I beg
> Your Majesty to watch with peaceful eye.

THE KING: (*wondering, aside*) Is it possible there is a subtext in the play?

XINYAN: (*sings*)

> All things in certain order are so made;
>
> For flowers there's a time to bloom, a time to droop.

XUELIAN: (*arises and sings*)

> With motions of the sun and moon the universe
> begins,

(THE KING *is shocked at this, as are all the lords.*)

XINYAN: (*sings*)

> And heav'n and earth come then to thrive and be.

XUELIAN: (*sings*)

> Who's he that can control nature's strong ways?

XINYAN: (*sings*)

> Objectifying leads to classifying.

XUELIAN AND XINYAN: (*together, sing*)

> One's subjectivity is not for trade:
>
> Think twice before decisions we may make.

XINYAN: (*desperate*) No, I can't—

> (*sings*)
>
> Bear to see them tie the knot, full of joy,
>
> While secrets of my own I have to hide.
>
> Rather than being made a bride afar,
>
> It's better here my grim, sad life to end!

(*The sword drawn, she actually attempts to kill herself.*)

XUELIAN: (*snatching the sword*) Hold it!

THE KING: (*rushes onto the stage and holds* XINYAN *in his arms*)

Aiyaa!—Xinyan!

JI: Aiyaa! No!

OTHER LORDS: (*shocked, trying to stop* THE KING) No, Your
Majesty! This is just play-acting.

THE KING: (*to* XINYAN) You are not hurt, are you?

(*looking around, embarrassed*) We've forgotten ourself!

(*He lets go of* XINYAN.)

(*solemnly, to* JI) So this is the romantic comedy my Lord
Chamberlain promised?

JI: (*terrified*) Your Majesty, what your humble servant promised
was . . . *What Good Luck!*. Somehow it's turned out to be
Confusion upon Confusion.— The play was (*quickly
shifting the blame*) specifically commanded by Her
Highness.

THE KING: (*confused*) What is all this?

XUELIAN: Your Majesty, indeed I revised the original play—

(*sings*)

In marriage ranks and titles have no place.

By heaven are our matches made, not man.

Companionship can help affections grow,

Resulting in Grand Nature's happy bond.

(*walks to* XINYAN *and holds her hand*)

XINYAN: (*returning to the play, sings*)

By sea and mountain anyone may swear;

> **Sincerity is proved by promise kept.**
>
> **If love be true or false, 'tis hard to tell,**
>
> **If being separated has no sway.**

XUELIAN: (*sings*)

> **Alliance with Wuyou I did not choose,**

XINYAN: (*sings*)

> **And to be forced is a pathetic state.**

XUELIAN: (*sings*)

> **In dreams I linger far away in hills,**

XINYAN: (*sings*)

> **But where's the paradise, the Shangri-la?**

(*All are surprised.*)

THE KING: (*solemnly*) What exactly do you mean?

XUELIAN: Your Majesty, it's my brother king's command that I come here to be your queen, and I could only comply. And yet . . .

THE KING: Well?

XUELIAN: To Your Majesty's great favor, I am much bound in gratitude. But destined love has nothing to do with fame or profit, and kindness is not equivalent to love. For two countries to strike an alliance by marriage, without the consent of the persons involved, is just inhuman. I crave Your Majesty's understanding.

THE KING: But such an alliance ensures friendship between our countries, begets posterity and guarantees lasting peace.

XUELIAN: Friendship between countries should be based on honest dealing and cooperation. Why force a living person against her will? If one has to put on an appearance of happiness unwillingly, what kind of life would that be? It's even worse than that of a character in a play!

JI: My most sagacious lord, women are ignorant. All they need to do is to obey traditional rules. Never let them speak up, nor be listened to. Otherwise we're in trouble.

THE KING: (*to* JI, *harshly*) Keep your mouth shut!

(*to* XUELIAN) Well—what then would Your Highness suggest?

XUELIAN: Your Majesty—

(*sings*)

> **All things cannot be treated the same way;**
> **Our situations vary case to case.**
> **Behaving like a puppet leads to rue;**
> **I only ask for precious liberty.**
> **The play within unfolds the problem's root:**
> **Let him who tied the bell untie it, please.**

THE KING: (*meditating*) Well—

JI: Your Majesty, alliances made by marriage have been practiced since time immemorial. For the princess to renege on the contract is ridiculous and unheard of!

OTHER LORDS: (*abuzz with comments*) Yes, that's right! The marriage must not be disavowed, or the consequences are unthinkable!

XUELIAN: Your Majesty, when has ever an unwilling alliance by marriage been successful? It's out of utter necessity that I devised this ill-advised plan. I beg that Your Majesty to think it over.

JI: When this news is spread, wouldn't it cause a huge scandal for Wuyou? Your Majesty mustn't yield to her.

XUELIAN: When this news is spread, all the world will know your boundless kindness. Such magnanimity will surely bring Your Majesty great fortune afterwards.

(*She walks to* XINYAN *and takes her hand.*)

(*to* THE KING, *sings*)

> **Haven't you heard—**
> **"A priceless treasure is obtained**
> **More easily than true, devoted love?"**
> **When you and she, who kindred spirits share,**
> **Are matched, immortal gods you will disdain.**

JI: (*to the audience*) I knew it! Once you let a woman open her mouth, she'll turn the whole world topsy-turvy!

OTHER LORDS: (*shocked, in noisy confusion*) Absolutely not! Absolutely not! This contradicts ethics. Absolutely impermissible!

THE KING: Alas—

(*sings an aside*)

True it is—

Traditional ethics as foundation firm

Have been handed down from ancestors.

True it is—

This alliance will be seen

As something good by foreign guest.

But yet—

She has declined the match with force;

And her argument is eloquent.

Alas for me—

I've lost my words; my tongue seems tied.

To have it both ways there's no easy way.

(*musing*)

(*looking at* XUELIAN, *sings*)

I cannot bear to see her—

In Wuyou stay, her heart remaining in her home.

(*looking at* XINYAN, *sings*)

I cannot bear to see her—

Ascend the tower, looking vainly through her tears.

(*looking at* XUELIAN, *sings*)

> I cannot bear to see her—
>
> Depressed and joyless, wishes all unmet.

(*looking at* XINYAN, *sings*)

> I cannot bear to see her—
>
> Forlorn and empty through the night.

(*after slight pause, sings*)

> This side, the heavy burden of the state;
>
> That side, one that haunts day and night.

(*after slight pause, sings*)

> Accomplished strategist, I know not what to do,
>
> But hesitate between this way and that.
>
> One false step may create a precedent,
>
> And too late in the future to recant. . . .

JI: Your Majesty, this Miss Xinyan is a mere player. Her abject status just doesn't fit . . .

OTHER LORDS: For the sake of peace, we must have this alliance! The royal marriage ceremony should go on as planned!

THE KING: Well—

XUELIAN: Your Majesty, if this alliance by marriage is unavoidable, so be it.—But please allow me first to take Xinyan back to my country.

THE KING: What? Your Highness . . . ?

(*The lords are all shocked.*)

XUELIAN: I mean to adopt Xinyan as my sister, and request my brother king to confer the royal title of princess on her. Ah, Your Majesty—

(*sings*)

> **Our social rank is not for us to choose:**
> **There will be gains and losses in our life.**
> **In moments grief may thus true joy become,**
> **And stifle all regrets in years to come.**
> **A happy royal match may you expect**
> **When flowers bloom in spring next year—**
> **That would be time for laughter and for wine!**

THE KING: Ah! Your Highness means—?

XUELIAN: Next year Your Majesty may come in person to take Xinyan, Princess of Zixu, home for your royal consort!

THE KING: (*touched*) Your Highness, (*bows*) we are much indebted to you!

XINYAN: (*kneels*) I humbly thank Your Highness!

XUELIAN: From now on, our two countries—

THE KING: Wuyou and Zixu shall be like brothers for ever and ever!

ALL LORDS: Congratulations! Congratulations! Congratulations, Your Majesty! Congratulations, Miss Xinyan!

(*Everybody freezes.*)

(*Light dims.*)

Epilogue

(Words projected on the screen: Half a Year Later)

[Offstage]: Set off!

> *(The royal retinue stately sets off from Wuyou.)*

[Chorus, offstage]:

> **Departed fall has springtime ushered in.**
>
> **Old friends he'll visit, an old theme to broach.**
>
> **So all the world is like a stage indeed,**
>
> **With entrances and exits all prescribed.**
>
> **To separate, rejoin, is destiny**
>
> **Whose endings may be happy or unapt.**
>
> **Give thoughtful empathy a chance to work,**
>
> **And lasting matrimony just may come to pass—**
>
> **It just may!**

The End

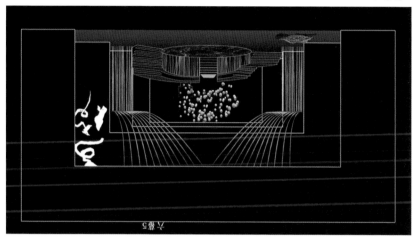

六幕5

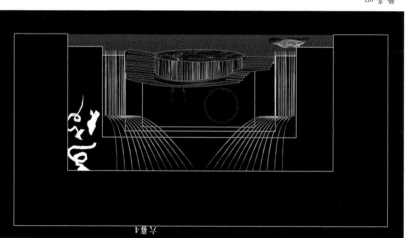

六幕4

可　待

（源自莎士比亞《皆大歡喜》）

彭鏡禧　著
陳　芳

臺灣 學生書局 印行

國家圖書館出版品預行編目資料

可 待

彭鏡禧、陳芳著. – 初版. – 臺北市：臺灣學生，2019.09
面；公分

ISBN 978-957-15-1813-8 (平裝)

863.54   108015111

可 待

著 作 者　彭鏡禧、陳芳
著作權所有　彭鏡禧、陳芳 cueariel@gmail.com
出 版 者　臺灣學生書局有限公司
發 行 人　楊雲龍
發 行 所　臺灣學生書局有限公司
地　　　址　臺北市和平東路一段 75 巷 11 號
劃 撥 帳 號　00024668
電　　　話　(02)23928185
傳　　　眞　(02)23928105
E - m a i l　student.book@msa.hinet.net
網　　　址　www.studentbook.com.tw
登記證字號　行政院新聞局局版北市業字第玖捌壹號
定　　　價　新臺幣三〇〇元
出 版 日 期　二〇一九年九月初版
I S B N　978-957-15-1813-8

85405
有著作權 • 侵害必究

ISBN 978-957-15-1813-8

《可待》客家大戲版由榮興客家採茶劇團首演

日期：2019 年 10 月 5-6 日

地點：臺灣臺北市國家戲劇院

劇本原創	彭鏡禧、陳芳
客語版改編	榮興客家採茶劇團

導演	陳　樂
副導演	黃俊琅
鄔西王	蘇國慶
雪蓮	江彥瑮
姬總管	胡宸宇
梅團長	胡毓昇
心妍	陳芝后
莫愁	吳代真
天珩	陳思朋
賀伯	杜柏諭
荳蔻	劉姿吟
全椒	陳怡婷
緋櫻	陳怡如
音樂設計	鄭榮興
服裝設計	蔡毓芬
舞臺設計	高明龍
燈光設計	袁　文

序：莎劇變態演戲曲

鄭培凱

耶魯大學博士，著名詩人、書法家、精通詞曲

現任香港非物質文化遺產*諮詢委員會主席

　　臺灣好友彭鏡禧與陳芳，精研中外戲劇，特別對莎士比亞戲劇的中譯及改編有其特識，曾經聯手創作，以傳統中國戲曲的形式，改編莎劇故事，讓演員在舞臺上呈現四功五法，展示唱做俱佳的表演。故事的原型是莎士比亞劇作，舞臺的展演卻完全是中國的唱作念打，不但唱的是傳統花雅曲調，舉手投足都是程式化的身段，偶爾還穿插些龍套的翻滾、虎跳、前撲、小翻，甚至出現雲裡翻、鷂子翻身那樣的高難動作，惹得觀眾鼓掌叫好。這與莎劇在西方的演出形式，已經完全不同，可稱之為莎劇表演的藝術「變態」。

　　我用「變態」兩字，形容舞臺表演的藝術轉型，是有深意

---

*陳芳案：鄭教授認為「非物質文化遺產」（intangible cultural heritage）宜改譯為「非實物文化傳承」。

的，強調了東西方戲劇各有其演劇傳統，故事可以襲用，表演形式則迥然不同。西方的莎劇演出傳統，主流是話劇形式，雖然吐字咬腔講究特殊的抑揚頓挫，但畢竟不是載歌載舞的舞臺表演，更別說戲曲遵循的「有聲皆歌，無動不舞」了。即使是改編莎劇成歌劇或芭蕾形式，有唱有跳，也都各循其特殊的演藝傳統，與中國的戲曲大異其趣。因此，以戲曲形式展演莎劇故事，的確是文化傳統與藝術形式的「變態」。

說到文化傳統的變態，不禁令人想到日本江戶時代儒學學者林春勝（號鵞峰）與其子林信篤（號鳳岡）所編的《華夷變態》一書。這本書編於明清易代之際，主要記錄了滿清入關，取代明朝的中華正統，是蠻夷改變了華夏，是天崩地裂的歷史文化現象。林春勝在 1674 年（延寶二年）所撰序言中寫道：「崇禎登天，弘光陷虜，唐、魯才保南隅，而韃虜橫行中原，是華變於夷之態也。」從日本旁觀的角度看中原板蕩，除了觀察到改朝換代的紛亂，發現滿清入關後南方依然擾攘不定，有鄭成功的反清復明活動，有三藩之亂，鹿死誰手還在未定之際。但是，日本學者已經十分感慨「華夷變態」的情況，是文化發展的「非常態」。

這種「文化變態」現象，到了二十世紀，因為西方列強「諸夷」的侵略與西方文化的東漸，更在東方出現了井噴式的「用夷變夏」趨勢，甚至導致中國精英階層呼籲「全盤西化」。莎劇在中國的流行與演出，也基本遵循西方的話劇形式，成為中國戲劇界的主流演出方式。一直到二十世紀末期，以傳統戲曲形式演出莎劇，才逐漸在演藝界占有一席之地，有了京劇、崑曲、豫劇、粵劇各個劇種，在舞臺上展演莎劇故事。因此，就中國傳統戲曲

的演出而言，演出莎劇是一種「演藝變態」；而就莎劇的主流表演形式而言，莎劇在中國的戲曲演出也是一種「文化變態」。放在二十一世紀全球化趨勢之中來看，則是無可避免的文化交流與藝術融匯現象，變態或許就成了可持續的非常態。

近來彭鏡禧與陳芳又改編了莎劇故事，推出一齣《可待》，以傳統戲曲的形式搬上舞臺。有趣的是，這次改編的動作很大，故事情節取材自不同的莎劇劇本，有《皆大歡喜》（*As You Like It*）的片段，有《仲夏夜之夢》（*A Midsummer Night's Dream*）的片段，還穿插了《哈姆雷》（*Hamlet*）劇中劇的橋段，簡直像陸象山「六經註我，我註六經」，倒是別開生面。劇本文辭的創作，則毫不依傍莎劇原文的中譯，而是遵循中國傳統曲文的格式，展現情節的發展，讀起來就像傳奇戲文。這種劇本撰寫的轉化過程，是化莎劇為中國戲曲的「變態」，使得舞臺呈演不至於出現劇本文辭與表演程式的扞格，讓觀眾感到看的是戲曲，而非拼湊不中不西的戲詞，演出不倫不類的莎劇，感受不明不白的跨境演出。

且舉《可待》開頭的一段為例，演鄔西國王賞賜禮物給雪蓮公主，派遣宮女呈送寶物，唱詞如下：

宮女甲：（捧金盤過場，唱）珍珠雙環八寶鍊，

雪　　蓮：（接唱）我一生愛好是天然。

宮女乙：（捧銀盤過場，接唱）五色雲霞織錦緞，

雪　　蓮：（接唱）素服淡妝久經年。

熟悉崑曲的觀眾，一眼便可看出，這樣的戲詞是有所本的，靈感並非來自莎士比亞，而是來自湯顯祖《牡丹亭》的《驚夢》一折，演杜麗娘走出香閨，出現在小庭深院，唱【醉扶歸】一曲：

> 你道翠生生出落的裙衫兒茜，艷晶晶花簪八寶填。可知我常一生兒愛好是天然，恰三春好處無人見。

莎士比亞與湯顯祖地下有知，當撫掌頷首，讚歎二十一世紀東西文化的糅合，以湯公文辭演述莎翁故事，搬上戲曲舞臺，居然變態變得順暢，不顯山不露水，圓融流行，皆大歡喜。

這齣戲還利用不同劇團分別上場的安排，混搭了不同的戲曲劇種，演出崑劇、搖滾京劇（或嘻哈京劇、京劇歌唱劇），出現了解構性的戲曲展演，讓莎劇出現多重「變態」，呈現當前中國戲曲演藝的後現代追求，不但衝決網羅，融合中西，而且多元多樣，大膽創新，也算是莎劇中國化與本土化的努力吧。

〔弁言〕

「談情・說愛」以後

　　《可待》是一齣從莎士比亞《皆大歡喜》（*As You Like It*）發想，運用互文和後設手法，來探討愛情本質與人生自主的新戲。同時，也藉戲中戲的扮演，概略反映臺灣當代的劇場生態。

　　在《皆大歡喜》中，莎士比亞揭露了各種以「愛」為名的面向。不論最初的動機是情欲、犧牲、想像或衝動，這些融合「傷心、柔弱、善變、渴望、喜愛、傲慢、荒誕、愚蠢、淺薄、花心，以淚洗面、一臉歡顏——各種情緒都有一些，卻沒有一樣是真真實實的」表現，正好印證了試金石（Touchstone）的觀察：「就如同世上萬物難免一死，世上的情人因他們的愚昧而顯出人性」（". . . as all is mortal in nature, so is all nature in love mortal in folly." 2.4.43-44）；亦如本劇中賀伯所發議論：「愛情原本就是瘋瘋癲癲」。但世間應該還有一種愛情，不一定局限於男女之間，無關乎對錯得失，甚至不必言語，就這樣安安靜靜地凝望。即使過程曲折或沒有報償，也能昇華至某種境界，以同理心「護持、成全」對方真正的願望。而這種心意，乃是浮華人間最溫暖美麗的一抹光影，彰顯了某種個人堅定的信念價值；這才是人生值得追尋的「愛」。

　　所以，經由偽裝和角色扮演，本劇的外戲與戲中戲相互呼應。「談情‧說愛」以後，在主題上，外戲的雪蓮與（主要）戲中戲的心妍／桔梗其實是一體兩面——唯其自主，才有可能得到自由與真愛。至於全劇轉化諸多莎劇愛情名言，或以京劇、搖滾京劇、崑劇等不同劇種及劇團演出戲中戲，並透過戲劇情境來論辯生活與劇場，則是我們立足於臺灣當代社會的一種省思。希望所有的參與者，都能從戲劇活動中得到因應現實生活的智慧和啟示。

　　非常感謝鄭培凱教授為本書作序。好友呂柏伸兄雖未執導本劇，卻閱讀了初稿，提供許多寶貴的意見；陳樂導演也在具體討論和實踐中，見證了本劇的七稿修改史。他們的隆情厚誼，是我們感激不盡的。而鄭榮興總監和榮興客家採茶劇團的襄助，使《可待》在等待中仍有期待，於此一併深致謝忱。

目　錄

可　待

源自莎士比亞《皆大歡喜》

彭鏡禧、陳芳

人物表

鄔西王	鄔西國國王
雪蓮	紫夒國公主
姬總管	鄔西國王宮總管
梅團長	梅劇團團長
心妍	梅劇團優伶，主演格林國桔梗公主（鈴蘭之姐），後著男裝改扮農舍主人甄即事
莫愁	梅劇團優伶，主演格林國鈴蘭公主（桔梗之妹），後改扮村姑甄即期
天珩	梅劇團優伶，主演格林國世家子谷連天，新科狀元
賀伯	梅劇團優伶，主演格林國王宮弄臣優哈
辛團長	辛劇團團長，兼演汴梁城花花公子胡寶、優哈
荳蔻	辛劇團優伶，兼演小雅、辛大爺之妻辛娘子
全椒	辛劇團優伶，兼演小桃、辛娘子之丫鬟
唐團長	唐劇團團長，兼演阿德
緋櫻	雪蓮之貼身宮女

·可　待·

大臣若干人
侍衞若干人
宮女若干人

場 目

序 曲

（上舞臺紗幕後光影朦朧，鄔酉軍勝紫嫛軍，插旗山頭）

【幕後伴唱】：角聲吹月流星劍，
　　　　　　　三千鐵騎奏凱旋。
　　　　　　　邊關突襲一朝變，
　　　　　　　鄔酉屬國非當年。
　　　　　　　紫嫛君臣細盤點，
　　　　　　　安撫南疆賜紅顏──

（燈亮，下接第一場）

第一場　問情

（鄔酉國王宮，雪蓮寢宮外廳）

雪　蓮：（內唱）彩雲冉冉依山盡——
　　　　（緩上，入座，接唱）紅葉飄零花木深。
　　　　　　　　　　　　　　故國依稀夢中近，
　　　　　　　　　　　　　　黯然悲吟憶萱親。
　　　　　　　　　　　　　　綺麗年華青春夢，
　　　　　　　　　　　　　　遽然斷送淚紛紛。
　　　　（緋櫻持茶盤上，取茶置几上，侍立於後）
　　　　　　　　　　　　　　奉命和親贈禮品，
　　　　　　　　　　　　　　恨不生作男兒身。
【畫外音】：大王恩賞！
　　　　（眾宮女捧各色禮物輪上，展示於雪蓮前）
宮女甲：（捧金盤過場，唱）珍珠雙環八寶鍊，
雪　蓮：（接唱）我一生愛好是天然。
宮女乙：（捧銀盤過場，接唱）五色雲霞織錦緞，
雪　蓮：（接唱）素服淡妝久經年。
宮女丙：（捧玉盤過場，接唱）流蘇滿綴玲瓏扇，
雪　蓮：（接唱）何似雋永一詩篇。
宮女丁：（捧冰盤過場，接唱）六曲屏風溫涼盞。
雪　蓮：（接唱）繡房權作書房看。

（姬總管上，示意宮女戊捧鈿盒上）

姬總管：公主，（奉承地）還有這金釵鈿盒……

雪　蓮：（未看一眼，揮手）下去吧！

　　　　（接唱）遙望紫嬰終長嘆，

　　　　　　　　心懷憂懼圖周全。

　　　　（姬總管取過鈿盒，示意宮女戊下）

姬總管：（呈上）公主，大王他——

雪　蓮：（冷冷地）你也下去吧！

姬總管：這……

【畫外音】：大王駕到！

　　　　（鄔酉王上，姬總管迎上表示無奈，雪蓮起身，攜緋櫻
　　　　施禮）

　　　　（姬總管退到一旁）

鄔酉王：（向雪蓮）公主一件都不喜歡嗎？

雪　蓮：大王，鄔酉一向臣服於紫嬰，年年進貢不曾輕慢。而今
　　　　大王初立，竟奇襲制勝，四方震動。為安民心，王兄不
　　　　願輕啟戰端，故此遣嫁，雪蓮敢不從命？大王厚賜，實
　　　　是受之有愧。但不知大王將如何處置敗軍？

鄔酉王：呀，公主言重了——

　　　　（唱）我鄔酉與紫嬰相交多年，

　　　　　　　原來是兄弟邦互有往還。

　　　　　　　遇挑釁生嫌隙干戈難免，

　　　　　　　不得已為疆域搶占機先。

　　　　　　　令王兄既議和各自回轉，

　　　　　　從今後名分定四境均安。

雪　蓮：（拜下）多謝大王。

鄔酉王：（扶起，接唱）賢公主歸鄔酉黎民樂見，

　　　　　　　　孤王我奉上賓大局顧全。

　　　　　　　　珍奇寶但博取佳人一粲，

　　　　　（向姬總管白）拿過來。

　　　　　（姬總管向前，國王取金釵為雪蓮插上）

　　　　　（接唱）金步搖更平添三分媚妍。

姬總管：（笑臉奉承）可不是麼！御花園的紅牡丹也比不上哪！

雪　蓮：（旁唱）縱然是獨邀寵君恩匪淺，

　　　　　　　　也難解長相思飛度關山。

　　　　　　　　家國雖遠心不遠，

　　　　　　　　豈能因循隨方圓？

　　　　　　　　補天尚待密針線，

　　　　　　　　紅燭蠟盡心熬煎。

鄔酉王：總管，再過一旬，即是佳期，婚慶大典籌備得如何？

姬總管：一切按部就班進行，請大王放心。

雪　蓮：（忽然打斷）大王，雪蓮身體不適，忽感頭疼。

鄔酉王：（關切）莫不是著涼了？

　　　　　（向姬總管）快傳太醫！

姬總管：是。（欲下）

雪　蓮：（攔阻）不用，稍事休息即可，請容雪蓮先行告退。

鄔酉王：當真無礙？

雪　蓮：不妨，多謝大王。

鄔酉王：那……公主好生休息，孤王稍後再來探望。

　　　　（雪蓮低首施禮，下）

鄔酉王：（向緋櫻）小心侍候！

緋　櫻：是。（隨下）

鄔酉王：（目送公主背影）總管，自公主入宮以來，你們服侍可好？

姬總管：謹遵大王吩咐，四十八名宮女日夜輪流侍候，不敢怠慢一分。

鄔酉王：飲食日用如何？

姬總管：日常所需，件件比照長公主。

鄔酉王：嗯？那你說說看，公主為何總是悶悶不樂？

姬總管：這……或許是因紫夐國遠在北方，公主奉命嫁來鄔酉，事出突然。是以水土不服，思鄉情切。

鄔酉王：哦，是這樣嗎？

姬總管：大王，您對公主禮遇有加，無人不知。昨日您不是還特別指派工匠，依照紫夐王宮的樣式，要給公主蓋座別館嗎？待等別館落成，公主必然歡喜，不會再愁眉苦臉了。

鄔酉王：（沉吟）別館落成，總還有段時日。先要想個法子讓公主開心……

姬總管：（恭敬）是。啟稟大王，微臣打聽到公主在紫夐喜好觀賞戲劇，常與優伶往來。（試探）梅劇團的那位心妍姑娘演得極好，是否先傳她來唱兩齣給公主解解悶？

鄔酉王：（沉思）心妍……

姬總管：（察覺有異，趕忙岔開）或者召集咱們鄔酉的劇團競演

一番，微臣從中挑選一團，在婚慶大典上演出精彩愛情
喜劇，給公主一個大大的驚喜。微臣保證，公主看了戲，
發現我國的藝文水準這麼高，一定心花怒放。

鄔酉王：這……可行嗎？

姬總管：大王，您看，微臣很少提出「保證」。可一旦「保證」
了，幾曾失誤？

鄔酉王：（想一想）那倒不曾。

姬總管：（指著己頭）微臣敢以這顆腦袋作保，這回也錯不了。

鄔酉王：（遲疑）好吧，你可要仔細了。

姬總管：遵命。（面露得色）為君分憂，微臣萬幸。微臣這就去
辦。（下）

鄔酉王：心妍……唉！

（切光）

【過場】

（小光區）

（姬總管上）

姬總管：大王有旨，演戲祝釐。經過老夫初選，列位都是獲得第
一階段賞金的劇團。只要演得好，就能拿到第二階段的
賞金。不但大王會指派重量級編劇來指導精修劇本，在
婚慶大典上獻演；還可以納編為「國王劇團」，入駐王

宮劇場。大家務須小心在意！（下）
　　　　（梅、唐、辛團長依序急上、急下）

梅團長：（唱）上頭傳話要演戲，
　　　　　　看看光景日偏西。
　　　　　　三步併作兩步走，
　　　　　　排練不知渴與飢。

唐團長：（接唱）上頭傳話要演戲，
　　　　　　就我一個人不齊。
　　　　　　拿手劇目難尋覓，
　　　　　　熱鍋螞蟻心著急。

辛團長：（接唱）上頭傳話要演戲，
　　　　　　討好公主稱第一。
　　　　　　創新何必循舊例，
　　　　　　這回改編先出奇。

第二場　言情

（排練場）

（各劇團排練，眾演員集訓暖身，做各式戲曲動作，如劈叉、汗水、探海、跌撲……）

辛團長：（唱搖滾京劇）有人天生大富貴，

　　　　　　　　　　有人努力才富貴，

　　　　　　　　　　有人憑空得富貴，

　　　　　　　　　　張開雙臂、勇敢擁抱最可貴。

唐團長：（唱崑劇）【山桃紅】（則為你）如花美眷，似水流年，

　　　　是答兒閒尋遍。在幽閨自憐。……

（梅團長上）

梅團長：趕緊、趕緊，開排了！姬總管來了！

　　　　（心妍飾桔梗著男裝改扮甄即事、莫愁飾鈴蘭改扮甄即期、賀伯飾優哈入戲。梅團長招呼姬總管入座，其他人下）

心　妍：（唱）如花美眷喬裝扮，

莫　愁：（接唱）姐妹離宮避禍端。

心　妍：（接唱）流年似水暗中換，

莫　愁：（接唱）苦等父王轉回還。

賀　伯：（白）桔梗公主、鈴蘭公主……

莫　愁：（搶白）優哈，你又錯了！現在姐姐改扮男裝，是農舍
　　　　主人甄即事，本宮是村姑甄即期。你可要記牢了。

賀　伯：是是是。少爺、小姐，大王出訪契丹，一時之間是不會
　　　　回京的。

心　妍：（接唱）須防繼母好手段，

　　　　　　　　囑託奶娘消息傳。

　　　　（白）優哈，你先給靳嬤嬤送個信去，附耳上來——
　　　　（低聲交代，賀伯不斷點頭）懂了嗎？

賀　伯：是。

　　　　（天珩飾谷連天肩背行囊上）

心　妍：別作聲！有人來了。你們先迴避吧。

　　　　（莫愁、賀伯下）

天　珩：（拱手）這位小哥，請問此處是阿里森林麼？

心　妍：（拱手）是。（打量天珩，旁白）此人好像谷兄……但
　　　　他這身打扮……？

　　　　（白）在下甄即事，請問閣下怎麼稱呼？

天　珩：在下谷連天，幸會了。

心　妍：（一驚，旁白）果然是他！

　　　　（強作鎮定）啊，谷兄莫不是今年皇榜開科的狀元郎？
　　　　令尊乃兩朝元老谷太師，真乃簪纓世族。

天　珩：謬讚了。我看甄兄談吐不俗，不像鄉野中人。難道曾供
　　　　職朝廷，認識先父？

心　妍：（急忙）不、不，小弟世居於此，只不過有位叔父通曉

礼仪，熟知世務。承他教導，小弟對朝中大事略知一二。
冒昧請教，谷兄因何來此？

天　珩：唉，說來慚愧——

（唱）先父墳塋尚未冷，

　　　　兄長襲爵已不容。

　　　　考場奪魁雖僥倖，

　　　　殺機四伏暗心驚。

（白）若非老僕相救，在下早已命喪黃泉，焉能到此？

心　妍：竟有此事！何不稟明君上？

天　珩：大王出京，朝中無人做主，在下只能先避一避了。

（接唱）人生無端造化弄，

　　　　　波濤洶湧意難平。

（白）聽說阿里森林聚集不少綠林好漢，首領摩白門為
家父舊友，故來投奔。

心　妍：谷兄啊——

（唱）虛矯繁華南柯夢，

　　　　日履薄冰盜聲名。

　　　　何如流連四時景，

　　　　原野百合任枯榮。

天　珩：（接唱）山居歲月誰與共？

心　妍：（接唱）鳥語花香笑相迎。

天　珩：（接唱）松柏能言泉下影？

心　妍：（接唱）萬物靜觀自分明。

（白）谷兄不必灰心，縱然令兄不顧手足之情，仍有老

僕耿耿忠心。何況摩首領慷慨豪俠，仁義為先，谷兄在
此定會賓至如歸。

天　珩：多謝甄兄寬慰。

心　妍：自己人毋須客套。

天　珩：自己人？

心　妍：（掩飾）哦，是啊，四海之內皆兄弟嘛，都是自己人。
　　　　（熱切）此去摩首領處尚有三里路，小弟願為前導。

天　珩：有勞了。

　　　　（心妍、天珩圓場，繼續無聲演出）

姬總管：梅團長，你說這齣戲是什麼來著？

梅團長：（陪笑）回稟大人，這是《錯中錯》。經過一連串的巧
　　　　合、誤會，最後有情人終成眷屬啊。

姬總管：這劇名不好！犯忌諱！

梅團長：啊？

姬總管：大王即將大喜，何錯之有？這《錯中錯》……

梅團長：大人，您老給我們指導指導，我們可都仰仗您了。

姬總管：嗯──就叫《好彩頭》吧，更適合咱們鄔西文化。

梅團長：（極力阿諛）大人改得好、改得好！改得好極了、好極
　　　　了，真是切題啊！

姬總管：（得意）這婚慶祝釐可馬虎不得！大王的心思更要好好
　　　　琢磨！

梅團長：是、是，大人說得是……

（心妍走入上場門）

天　珩：（從袖中取筆，轉身在竹上題詩）

　　　　（唱）林間書寫纏綿意，

　　　　　　　祇緣當年種相思。

　　　　　　　惆悵天涯存知己，

　　　　　　　萍聚究竟待何時？

　　　　（賀伯閒逛上，看詩）

　　　　　　　雙魚欲寄無從寄，

　　　　　　　詩題琅玕有情癡。

賀　伯：哈！我當是誰，原來是個白癡在這裡畫樹皮！

天　珩：錯了，是情癡在書寫情詩哪。

賀　伯：（向觀眾）情癡，就是白癡嘛，對不對？愛情原本就是
　　　　瘋瘋癲癲。

　　　　我來看看您又寫了什麼？

　　　　（吟誦）懷疑星星是火燄，

　　　　　　　懷疑太陽會挪移，

　　　　　　　懷疑真理是謊言，

　　　　　　　不可懷疑我愛你。

　　　　（向谷）這是詩？您作的？（調侃）好才情！

天　珩：非也，此乃丹麥國哈姆雷王子的詩作。在下心有同感，
　　　　順手引用罷了。

　　　　（指另一竿竹）這裡才是拙作。

賀　伯：（怪腔怪調吟誦）荒蕪總在離別後，

　　　　　　　　　　　片雲遮日……

天　珩：（打斷他）不是這種腔調，聽了——
　　　　（唱）荒蕪總在離別後，
　　　　　　　片雲遮日多煩憂。
　　　　　　　桃李爭豔自古有，
　　　　　　　心繫空谷一蘭幽。
　　　　　　　山村無處沽美酒，
　　　　　　　流水宛轉不自由。
　　　　　　　俯仰天地獨立久，
　　　　　　　不見伊人愁上愁。

賀　伯：（向觀眾）哎呀，這說的是什麼意思啊？
　　　　（向天珩）依小人看，還是丹麥那個什麼王子的詩更動
　　　　人，至少人人聽得明白。您就別再作詩糟蹋竹林了——
　　　　不環保啊。

天　珩：（拂袖）你也別再胡亂吟誦，糟蹋了本公子的好詩。

姬總管：（倏地站起）停！你們這演的是什麼？老夫可是在大王
　　　　面前保證過，一定要演精彩的愛情喜劇！

賀　伯：稟告總管大人，據說愛情花苞經過夏風吹熟，只等情人
　　　　下次相遇，就能開出美麗的花朵。小人演的是「夏風吹
　　　　花苞」這一段……
　　　　（梅團長急忙揮手，制止賀伯説下去）

梅團長：大人別心急啊！精彩的在下一段……

姬總管：哼！老夫怎能不心急？婚慶吉日眼看就要到了，你們才
　　　　排了一場，這小丑又不知在演什麼東西？

梅團長：哎呀，咱們梅劇團的演出，一向是有品質保證的。您老

又不是不知道，整個鄩西就只有咱們行當齊全。這會兒雖然排戲進度慢了點兒，但大夥兒都很專業，同心協力一股腦兒就排完了。您老過兩日再來瞧瞧，包準兒好看！

姬總管：（半信半疑）你不要誆哄老夫！這可不能開玩笑。若有半點差池，大王是絕對不會輕饒的。

梅團長：您老請放心，小的辦事一向認真，錯不了、錯不了……

姬總管：嗯，這竹林嘛，（指點）這裡、這裡、還有那裡，都得擺上幾竿竹子。喏，這裡也要加兩塊大石頭，才像真的。再弄幾個武行來翻筋斗，那才好看。祝釐嘛，就是要熱鬧，懂嗎？

梅團長：是是是，大人不愧是行家，說得對極了。

賀　伯：（向天珩）唉，這回恐怕是又要弄成個四不像啦！

天　珩：噓！小點聲兒。（苦笑）長官怎麼會有錯？

姬總管：老夫還要再交代幾句。

梅團長：是、是，您老請說。

姬總管：心妍姑娘呢？

梅團長：是、是。（向上場門高喊）心妍——

　　　　　（心妍急上）

心　妍：團長找我？

　　　　　（梅團長使眼色，指姬總管）

　　　　　（轉向姬）大人有何吩咐？

姬總管：心妍姑娘，你可要好好表現啊。雖說你常進宮演出，但這次可不比往常。大王寵愛雪蓮公主，非常重視這個婚慶祝釐戲。你是咱鄩西最好的優伶，務必打點精神，給

　　　　大王爭個臉面，不要讓公主小覷了咱們。

心　妍：是，心妍盡力。

姬總管：嗯嗯，好、好。

　　　　（向梅團長）時候不早了，老夫得去瞧瞧辛劇團，你們
　　　　加緊排戲吧。

梅團長：是、是，恭送大人。大人慢走、大人慢走……（梅送姬
　　　　下）

心　妍：（百感交集，旁白）沒想到——大王如此寵愛公主……
　　　　（旁唱）往事如煙堪重數，
　　　　　　　　孰知貴賤竟分殊。
　　　　　　　　但是相思莫相負，
　　　　　　　　一片冰心在玉壺。

　　　　（切光）

第三場　真情

（鄔酉國王宮，鄔酉王寢宮外廳）
（鄔酉王、雪蓮交談中，緋櫻侍立）

鄔酉王：（靦腆一笑）公主深夜來訪，原來為了此事。這演戲祝
　　　　釐，乃本王一片心意，原是要給公主一個驚喜。不料風
　　　　聲已然走漏。

雪　蓮：（微笑）感謝大王美意。這也是（指緋櫻）緋櫻剛好聽
　　　　聞奏報。（停頓）不知可否讓雪蓮來督導選戲？

鄔酉王：這——

雪　蓮：大王——
　　　　（唱）戲劇大觀我知曉，
　　　　　　　四功五法難度高。
　　　　　　　若非王命忽然報，
　　　　　　　紫嫕劇場正細瞧。

鄔酉王：（接唱）素聞公主心思巧，
　　　　　　　　戲理通達名兒標。
　　　　　　　　鄔酉劇團人數少，
　　　　　　　　此時琴絃尚未調。

雪　蓮：（接唱）風土迥異失歡笑，
　　　　　　　　閒坐宮闈亦無聊。

鄔酉王：（接唱）倉促成事恐貽笑，

醞釀方可去濁醪。

雪　蓮：（接唱）他鄉不如故鄉好——

鄔酉王：（旁白）呀！他鄉不如？既是這般——

　　　　（白）公主啊，你就——

　　　　（接唱）點評戲齣慰寂寥。

雪　蓮：（喜悦）謝大王！

　　　　大王公務繁忙，雪蓮告退。

　　　　（走到門外，雪蓮不慎掉落繡帕，與緋櫻同下）

鄔酉王：（自言自語）這位公主，著實不易取悅啊。

　　　　（欲批閱奏摺，卻又放下，移步回廊）

　　　　唉！（唱）宮牆高、回廊長，

　　　　（心妍喬裝上，張望著、閃避著）

心　妍：（接唱）過宮牆、繞回廊。

鄔酉王：（接唱）花徑深、月下望，

心　妍：（接唱）穿花徑、月昏黃。

鄔酉王：（接唱）三更思念意難忘，

心　妍：（接唱）三更潛行莫徬徨。

鄔酉王：（接唱）寒夜透涼無人講，

心　妍：（接唱）何懼寒意夜生涼。

　　　　（急行入宮，白）大王！

鄔酉王：（轉身，歡喜迎上）心妍，孤正思念著你，你就來了。

心　妍：（微笑）心妍與大王心意相通啊。

鄔酉王：唉——

　　　　（唱）想當初我本是庶出私生子，

少小牧羊在山林。

想當初卑微貧困乏人問，

惟有卿卿笑語親。

（二人陷入回憶）

鄔酉王：（接唱）若耶溪畔心相印，

高山流水奏雅音。

心　妍：（接唱）鰷魚忽然來遠近，

綠蔭低椏不礙雲。

鄔酉王：（接唱）輕煙細雨朦朧去，

心　妍：（接唱）且向蓼花深處尋。

（二人回到現實）

鄔酉王：（接唱）未料儲君天年盡，

大統承擔在我身。

（緋櫻上，沿路尋找）

緋　櫻：公主的繡帕到底在哪兒呢？（尋到宮門口）啊，在那兒！

（撿起繡帕，發現鄔酉王挽著心妍，掩藏偷聽）

鄔酉王：（接唱）小國寡民須用忍，

遵循祖制允大婚。

辜負卿卿潮無信，

愧對知心眼前人。

心　妍：（白）不不不，大王切莫如此──

（接唱）明君當以社稷重，

兒女私情置罔聞。

心妍取捨知分寸，

用心扮演戲中人。

祝釐之後歸鄉隱——

（白）其實我正是來拜別大王的，相信故里——

（接唱）蔥翠柳色一樣新。

鄔西王：（不禁擁抱）心妍……

緋　櫻：這唱的是哪一齣啊？我得趕快去向公主報告。（急下）

心　妍：大王——保重！

（切光）

【過場】

（鄔西國王宮，排練室）

（梅、辛二團上，眾優伶七嘴八舌，唐團長一人上）

梅團長：（向前，唱）黃金陣容萬事備，

辛團長：（向前，接唱）新腔新調新作為。

唐團長：（看看後面沒人，更向前，接唱）變通戲法人人會，

　　　　（姬總管上）

姬總管：（接唱）公主欽點我難發揮。

　　　　（白）老夫的差事換了主兒啦！

【畫外音】：公主駕到！

姬總管：你們都下去準備吧。

（下接第四版）

謎：　是。（下）

· 上午 ·

第四場　觀情

（鄔西國王宮，排練室）
（雪蓮上，緋櫻隨上）

雪　蓮：（唱）今朝奉旨點戲齣，
　　　　　　審時度勢自吟哦。
　　　　　　命運攸關非小可，
　　　　　　良謀切忌巧成拙。
　　　　　　昨宵聞報心有數，
　　　　　　欲罷婚宴易弦轍。
　　　　　　輾轉苦思萬全策，
　　　　　　正言若反宜斟酌。
　　　　　　且看眾生說因果，
　　　　　　細凝神、從中推敲太平歌。

（姬總管迎上施禮，雪蓮入座）

姬總管：啟稟公主，鄔西三大劇團競演即將開始。
　　　　（呈上戲單）這是各劇團的戲單。

雪　蓮：嗯。

（緋櫻上前接過，打開展示，雪蓮略瞄一眼，示意知道）
（以下各劇團輪番演戲。唐劇團演出崑劇，辛劇團演出搖滾京劇〔或嘻哈京劇、京劇歌唱劇〕，梅劇團演出京劇）

姬總管：啟稟公主，首先，唐劇團搬演崑劇《情奔仲夏夜》——
　　　　　小精靈錯點了愛情符水，使阿德睡醒後，愛上第一眼看
　　　　　到的小桃，完全忘記了私奔情人小雅……

緋　櫻：不須總管解說，公主熟知此劇。

姬總管：（一拍腦門）啊，該打，微臣竟忘了公主是內行。

雪　蓮：（微笑）有勞了。

姬總管：（向上場門）開演。

　　　　　（唐團長飾阿德、荳蔻飾小雅上「臺上臺」）

荳　蔻：（看看左右）唐團長，這是空臺耶？

唐團長：沒錯，這是極簡劇場——賞金這麼少，只夠做衣服，布
　　　　　景就靠想像了。

荳　蔻：哦哦。（入戲）阿德，奴家背棄嚴父，與君相約私奔。
　　　　　君何其忍心，竟棄我於此黝闇森林之中！

唐團長：（唱）【金瓏璁】深情將我喚，不覺浮想聯翩。
　　　　　（白）小桃美如夜空明月，令小生無法自已，只得趨行
　　　　　向前。小雅，昔日恩情已矣，切莫阻攔於我。

荳　蔻：（愁容滿面）不不不，君何其糊塗！是這片詭異山林魅
　　　　　惑了你，竟使君忘卻至愛！

唐團長：糊塗的是你。小生鍾情於小桃，永生無悔！小桃，小桃
　　　　　——小生來也！（下）

荳　蔻：不，阿德——（追下）

　　　　　（全椒飾小桃上，唐團長對面上）

唐團長：呀，來者豈非小桃？（奔上）卿卿吾愛！

全　椒：（受驚）阿德，君中邪否？奴家乃是小桃，並非小雅！

唐團長：小桃不要誤會，小生鍾情於你已然多時了——

（唱）【好事近】雲雨甚因緣，（看）嬌嬈向花間展。
（不提防）神魂顛倒，山盟海誓（多）情願。（似這般）
生生死死心心念念，由人戀。（早則是）情話綿綿，惟
見我志誠一片。（任憑他）星移斗轉，（但求得）花好
月圓。

全　椒：莫非嘲諷奴家麼？公子明知我所愛慕的米公子亦鍾情小
雅，對我視而不見。奴家已陷於萬劫不復，不該再引來
這番譏嘲吧？公子此言應對小雅說去。

唐團長：（急忙）小生發誓，自始至終，（指己心）只有卿卿，
別無他人。

全　椒：此亦誓言，彼亦誓言，相互抵銷，孰知真假？

唐團長：小生絕無半句虛言，卿卿何以不信？

全　椒：公子何須作弄於我？天啊，難道只因奴家愛上一個不愛
我的人，就活該被這般作弄麼？

（唱）【山水青】問月老……

（臺上臺繼續無聲表演）

雪　蓮：（心中一動，旁唱）情愛牽引任滋長，

盲目糾結空悲涼。

拘泥世俗誰做主？

隨波逐流無事忙。

小中見大非虛妄，

鍾情二字費思量。

　　　　　（臺上臺謝幕）

姬總管：（請示）公主，您看這戲怎麼樣？

雪　蓮：（回神）演得不錯，下去領賞吧。

　　　　　（姬總管揮手）

唐團長、全椒：謝公主。

　　　　　（全椒下）

唐團長：（拭汗，旁白）我這一人劇團，有面子、沒裡子。這次
　　　　　特別情商辛劇團的小花旦荳蔻、全椒來客串，蒙混過關，
　　　　　好僥倖啊！（下）

　　　　　（雪蓮示意緋櫻）

緋　櫻：總管，下一團演什麼？

姬總管：啟稟公主，接著是辛劇團的《辛貞女》——聽說是搖滾
　　　　　京劇。因為臨時換戲，微臣也尚未過目。辛團長強調這
　　　　　是歌頌淑女品德堅貞的好戲，請公主賞鑑。

緋　櫻：搖滾京劇？

雪　蓮：這倒新鮮。

姬總管：（向上場門）開演。

　　　　　（檢場搬一桌二椅上）

　　　　　（荳蔻飾辛娘子上，坐主位讀信；全椒飾丫鬟隨上，侍
　　　　　立；辛團長飾胡寶上）

辛團長：（唱）花花大爺俺叫胡寶，

　　　　　　　　汴梁城內聲名高。

　　　　　　　　無人不知、無人不曉，

　　　　　　　　青樓夜夜紅袖招。

前日來了個辛大少，

吹噓他老婆風姿嬌，

雞蛋大珍珠跟俺賭，

老子吳江走一遭。

（白）話說老子在酒肆巧遇吳江商賈辛大爺，幾杯黃湯下肚，他便以他老婆和俺打賭。若老子誘拐不到貞潔的辛娘子，就得輸掉夜明珠了。所以，（坐客位）閒話休提，老子就來送家書了。

荳　蔻：（把信折好）胡大爺，我夫君在汴梁生活狀況如何？

辛團長：（支吾）這個嘛……

荳　蔻：（不解）胡大爺有何為難？還請實告，切勿隱瞞。

辛團長：哎呀，俺真是替小娘子不值啊。

荳　蔻：呀，此話從何說起？

辛團長：論理俺不該在背後嚼舌根，說朋友是非，但他——

　　　　（唱）流連館閣攀花柳，

　　　　　　夜夜笙歌醉不休。

　　　　　　紅粉知己到處有，

　　　　　　吳江浪子出風頭。

荳　蔻：我夫君當真這麼放浪？

辛團長：那可不？俺真是可憐小娘子你喲——俺若能一親芳澤，摸摸這纖纖玉手，香香這粉臉蛋，絕不會像辛大爺那樣不知好歹，撇下自家手上的鑽石，反倒在外頭撿玻璃……

荳　蔻：這是何言語？太卑劣了！滾出去！奴家聽不下去了……

姬總管：（厲聲）停！老夫才聽不下去！

（辛、荳、全受驚，停止演戲）

（向公主）這亂七八糟不知演些什麼！真是丟祖師爺的臉面。公主見諒，微臣必會好好責罰辛劇團。

雪　蓮：（向辛）這是怎麼回事？

辛團長：（委屈）回稟公主，本團原來排演《悉聽尊意》，但總管大人說這犯了忌諱……

全　椒：（插嘴）就是韋奧拉姑娘苦戀伊利王，最後終成眷屬的喜劇……

雪　蓮：哦——？（轉向緋櫻，低聲）是這個？

緋　櫻：（低聲）不是，是梅劇團的心妍。

辛團長：（制止全椒）不准胡說。總之，大人命令咱們換戲。小的就想，《辛貞女》也不錯啊——不論這胡寶如何誘惑，辛娘子都堅守婦道，維護自己的清白……

姬總管：你還有詞兒？還敢狡辯？

辛團長：大人，小的句句實言，不敢欺瞞，求大人明察。為了趕排這齣新戲，本團可是日以繼夜，沒有片刻休息啊。

全　椒：（旁白）對，團長違反勞基法。

荳　蔻：（阻止）不要火上澆油。

雪　蓮：（向緋櫻）看來這齣戲反映了女子的悲哀。生為女子，竟然這般不得自由。嫁個夫君，好像做了主婦，其實還是個附屬品。

緋　櫻：是啊，人家隨便拿顆珍珠就可以交換，「以物易物」，著實可悲可嘆。辛娘子，一個傀儡嘛！

姬總管：（旁白）這——叫老夫如何回話？莫非公主……

（向公主）這辛劇團插科打諢也太不像話，微臣這就打
發了他們……

雪　蓮：總管，本宮自有主張。

姬總管：是。

雪　蓮：（向辛、荳、全）你們都先下去吧。

辛團長、荳蔻、全椒：謝公主。（下）

緋　櫻：（向公主）看來對祝釐戲不能期望太高。

姬總管：（尷尬）公主，也有編制相對較完整的劇團，比方這最
　　　　後壓軸的梅劇團——行政、演出、製作樣樣齊全，可謂
　　　　本國第一大團。

雪　蓮：是嗎？他們演什麼？

姬總管：《好彩頭》——

　　　　（緋櫻噗哧一笑，雪蓮示意不可）

　　　　（急忙）原名《錯中錯》，這可是微臣改的劇名。

雪　蓮：是取其吉祥之意吧？總管費心了。

姬總管：（得意）正是。梅劇團演的可是正規京劇。劇情是格林
　　　　國二位公主，在大王出訪期間，因被繼母迫害，匆忙帶
　　　　著弄臣優哈避居阿里森林。考量便於行事，姐姐桔梗公
　　　　主女扮男裝，成了農舍主人甄即事。剛好青梅竹馬的新
　　　　科狀元谷連天，也因避難逃往阿里，二人在此意外相
　　　　遇……

　　　　（雪蓮與緋櫻對看一眼，向姬做手勢）

　　　　開演。

　　　　（天珩飾谷連天在竹上題詩，心妍飾桔梗著男裝改扮甄

即事上）

心　妍：（微笑，看看竹）兄長真是好興致！

天　珩：賢弟取笑了。山野生活即便艱辛，也不能改變愚兄的真
　　　　情。

心　妍：兄長在這一大片竹林之上題詩，所為何來？

天　珩：唉，不瞞賢弟，愚兄心裡苦悶得很哪。

心　妍：（關切）哦？此話怎講？

天　珩：賢弟啊——

　　　　（唱）莫怪愚兄忒顛倒，

　　　　　　　刻骨相思苦難熬。

　　　　　　　風月消磨音書杳，

　　　　　　　聊訴深情竹林梢。

心　妍：（一驚，旁唱）記得當時年紀小，

　　　　　　　　　嬉戲宮苑時相招。

　　　　　　　　　也曾同覓忘憂草，

　　　　　　　　　重逢更訂金蘭交。

　　　　（念及與鄔酉王兩小無猜、相互扶持的時光，動情落淚，
　　　　急忙掩飾）難道紅繩繫月老，

　　　　　　　　　虧負前情各揚鑣？

雪　蓮：（旁唱）她那裡心跡昭然如月皎，

　　　　　　　　　分明是情深似海難輕拋。

心　妍：（旁白）我定要問個清楚！

雪　蓮：（旁白）我定要弄個明白！

心　妍：（白）敢問兄長，意中人兒是哪一個？

天　珩：這……我若說將出來，你可得保守秘密。

心　妍：小弟對天發誓，絕不洩露一字。

天　珩：是二字。

心　妍：哪二字？

天　珩：（低聲）桔——梗——

心　妍：（一呆）什麼？

天　珩：公主啊——

心　妍：（以為身分揭露，大驚）啊——

天　珩：（唱）我與公主、青梅竹馬情誼好，

　　　　　　　三年整、整三年，同窗共讀樂陶陶。

心　妍：（想到鄔西王，接旁唱）他與公主、兩國聯姻天下曉，

　　　　　　　祝釐戲、戲祝釐，真真假假紅燭燒。

天　珩：（接唱）我為公主、日日曉行宮牆道，

　　　　　　　漫漫長夜立中宵。

心　妍：（接旁唱）他為公主、興建別館投所好，

　　　　　　　故人情誼全勾消。

天　珩：（接唱）我只道、皇榜開科龍門躍，

　　　　　　　良緣早定眉黛描。

心　妍：（接旁唱）我只道地久天長江湖遨，

　　　　　　　良緣終究眉黛描。

天、心：（接同唱）孰料今日、浮名都拋，安身荒野人跡少，

　　　　　　　哪裡有對症良藥治心焦？

　　　　　（心妍悲傷恍神，天珩不得不提點她）

天　珩：（重唱）——治心焦？

心　妍：（回神，故作驚喜，接旁唱）忽聞兄長彈悲調，

全盤托出說根苗。

（正要吐實，轉念，旁白）且慢——

（接旁唱）操之過切驚弓鳥，

我還是——靜待他日冤情昭。

（白）兄長情深意摯，這位公主真是有福之人，小弟不
勝羨慕啊。

天　珩：（苦笑）羨慕什麼？公主全然不知此事，兼且分別多年，
縱使相見亦未必相識。

（心妍暗笑）

愚兄自導自演單相思，著實苦惱哇！

心　妍：（放心）兄長不必自苦。當今癡情公子少見得很，小弟
佩服。（思索）這麼著吧，小弟來尋個良方對付您這相
思病。

天　珩：什麼良方？果能解憂麼？

心　妍：沒問題，就讓小弟來扮演公主吧。

天　珩：啊？

（心妍繼續向天珩解釋，有身段、無聲音）

雪　蓮：（似有所悟，旁白）扮演公主？一帖良方……

（旁唱）任憑弱水過三千，

只取一瓢心意堅。

明知同行不是伴，

各自前程路更寬。

（旁白）與其由王兄做主，名為聯姻，實是逼嫁。任人

擺布，了無生趣。何不另闢蹊徑，藉戲說戲，或有一線
生機？再說這心妍……

　　（接旁唱）既然是生旦淨丑任點選，

　　　　　　　倒不如布置關目到御前。

　　　　　　　玄機暗藏乾坤轉，

　　　　　　　巧借祝釐吐真言。

　　　　　　　起承轉合開生面，

　　　　　　　戲劇結局要改觀。

　　　　　　　自編自導寓意遠，

　　　　　　　登天何懼蜀道難！

　　（打定主意，起身，白）罷了！今天就到此為止。

　　（天珩、心妍定格）

姬總管：啟稟公主，尚未演完啊，這鄔西三大劇團競演……

　　（梅團長衝上）

雪　蓮：嗯？

姬總管：啊，這是梅團長。（向梅）這麼沒規矩……

梅團長：公主恕罪、大人恕罪，小人一時情急，忘了禮數。因為
　　　　　本團彩排的精華，都在下一段啊。公主，這……

雪　蓮：（微笑，向梅）不必著急。

　　　　　（向姬）總管說得不錯，梅劇團優伶最佳。表演生動靈
　　　　　活，頗能傳情達意，很有感染力，不愧是鄔西第一大團。
　　　　　祝釐演戲的任務，就交由梅劇團承擔吧。

姬總管：公主果然好眼光。

梅團長：多謝公主！公主英明！

雪　蓮：本宮還沒說完。

梅團長：公主請吩咐，小人恭聆教訓。

雪　蓮：（緩慢）假如本宮想調整部分唱念，增減一些情節，不
　　　　會有問題吧？

姬總管：（驚訝）這……

梅團長：沒問題、沒問題，當然沒問題。能夠得到公主的青睞和
　　　　指導，是本團莫大的榮耀。小人必定全力以赴。

雪　蓮：很好。明日你們再來一趟，本宮有話交代。

梅團長：是、是，多謝公主！

雪　蓮：起駕！

　　　　（雪蓮、緋櫻、姬總管下）

梅團長：恭送公主！

　　　　（眾施禮）

　　　　（向天珩、心妍招手，天珩趨前）：明兒個進宮，你們
　　　　先去……（二人交談下）

心　妍：（旁白）不知公主是何主意？唉──

　　　　（旁唱）半是人生半是戲，

　　　　　　　　半掩半遮半自欺。

　　　　　　　　只怕真情藏不住，

　　　　　　　　紅氍毹上訴相思。

　　　　（切光）

〔中輟本〕

第五場　悟情

（鄔酉國王宮，排練室）

（梅劇團排戲，莫愁飾鈴蘭改扮甄即期上）

莫　愁：（閒逛四顧，唱）是真還似假，

　　　　　　　　　轉身已天涯。

　　　　　　　　　青山隱約瓜棚下，

　　　　　　　　　阡陌縱橫有農家。

　　　　　　　　　平野並非舊時畫，

　　　　　　　　　零星點綴野草花。

　　　　（看竹，接唱）夢中人、空牽掛，

　　　　　　　　　竹林深處聽鳴蛙。

　　　　（屈指算，感動，白）這可是第四十九竿竹了！

　　　　（賀伯飾優哈上）

賀　伯：好小姐，您怎麼逛到這兒來啦？少爺要我找您回去哩。

莫　愁：（興奮）優哈，你看到沒有？這些題詩，好深情啊。

　　　　（吟）「可憐黃花入塵土，魂斷不敢高聲哭」、「尋思
　　　　前情俱已往，幾度西風話淒涼」……真是動人極了。

賀　伯：好小姐，您沒聽說過嗎？愈是看來真切的情詩，其實愈
　　　　浮誇。箇中誓言，大多虛情假意，不必兌現啊。

莫　愁：你懂什麼！

賀　伯：唉，聰明人向來只准自個兒做傻事，卻不准傻子賣弄幾

句聰明話。

莫　愁：別鬧了！喂，你知道這些詩是誰作的？

賀　伯：這個作詩的，病得可厲害啦。

莫　愁：怎麼說？

賀　伯：就是那谷公子嘛。聽說他相思成疾，不得不常到咱們農
　　　　舍來……

莫　愁：（搶話）他不是來與姐姐切磋學問的麼？

賀　伯：相思也是一種學問，得好好研究。

莫　愁：（略一沉思，忽有所悟）莫非那谷公子對姐姐……

　　　　（雪蓮、緋櫻、梅團長持手稿上）

雪　蓮：（打斷莫愁，向梅團長）本宮就從這裡改起！梅團長，
　　　　你看如何？

梅團長：（看手稿，恭敬）是是是，小人這就排起來。

　　　　（向莫愁、賀伯招手，給他們部分手稿，比手畫腳）你
　　　　們兩個……就這樣……這樣……懂了吧？

　　　　（莫愁、賀伯頻頻點頭）

　　　　（心妍飾桔梗著男裝改扮甄即事上，梅團長迎上，給心
　　　　妍部分手稿）

心　妍：這就是——？

梅團長：這就是。以下都照著公主的新本走！

心　妍：（翻看手稿，自言自語）看這新本——我演的好像是……
　　　　另一個公主……

梅團長：（向莫愁、賀伯）來來來，你們從「相思」這裡重來一
　　　　遍。

賀　伯：（看手稿）相思也是一種學問，得好好研究。

莫　愁：（看手稿，略一沉思，忽有所悟）難怪他看來總是心事
　　　　重重，莫非對我……
　　　　（一笑）優哈，咱們這就回去吧。（跑下）

賀　伯：小姐，急什麼啊？等等我啊！小姐……（追下）

雪　蓮：（向梅團長）繼續排，本宮為桔梗公主填了新詞……
　　　　（莫愁持手稿上，梅團長迎上，二人在上右舞臺討論劇
　　　　本）

心　妍：（看手稿，唱）幾度登臨春歸去，
　　　　　　　　　　　閑散蹉跎遊華胥。
　　　　　　　　　　　回首忘卻舊時路，
　　　　　　　　　　　莫名織就稼穡圖。
　　　　　　　　　　　無人知我喬裝苦，
　　　　　　　　　　　惟恐韶華太飄忽。
　　　　　　　　　　　幽情一縷向誰訴？
　　　　　　　　　　　夜半獨對一燈孤……

雪　蓮：（向心妍，白）這裡要表現出一種莫名的愁緒，要注意
　　　　情感的強度。你還在戲外哪。

心　妍：（接唱）花開怎堪風雨妒，
　　　　　　　　　半入塵土、半隨流水去平蕪。

雪　蓮：（向心妍，白）這可不行。你的情感不真，再細膩點兒！

心　妍：（忍耐）是。（以下不時看手稿，入戲）唉！改扮下鄉
　　　　已有數月，雖說谷兄每日來訪，解我煩憂，但畢竟身分
　　　　未明，諸多不便。不知宮中現下是何光景？父王是否回

　　　　　宮？教人好生掛念！

雪　蓮：鈴蘭公主該上了！

　　　　　（莫愁跑上，以下雪蓮不時與梅團長低聲交談，指點人
　　　　　物）

莫　愁：（以下不時看手稿）姐姐、姐姐，您覺得谷公子這個人
　　　　　如何？

心　妍：怎麼忽然問起他來？

莫　愁：別管為什麼，就說說看嘛，您覺得他——？

心　妍：谷兄啊——

　　　　　（唱）谷兄他、劍眉星目才華好，

　　　　　　　　　骨格清奇人品高。

　　　　　　　　　谷兄他、說古論今頭頭是道，

　　　　　　　　　當代難得真英豪。

莫　愁：（接唱）遑論他、情有獨鍾人人曉，

　　　　　　　　　農舍往來不辭勞。

　　　　　　　　　魂縈夢繫知多少？

　　　　　　　　　竹林深處賦離騷。

心　妍：（接旁唱）芳心暗許比翼鳥，

雪　蓮：（介入，向心妍，白）情感疏離了，你不是芳心暗許嗎？

心　妍：（旁白）啊，公主怎麼一直挑剔我呢？

莫　愁：（接旁唱）只盼父王早回朝。

心　妍：（接唱）雨過天青祥瑞兆，

莫　愁：（陶醉，接唱）與谷郎、今生今世、永不離分樂逍遙。

心　妍：（大驚）什麼？你……

莫　愁：姐姐，實不相瞞，我對谷兄仰慕已久……（羞澀）回宮
　　　　以後，姐姐可否幫忙向父王說項？

心　妍：（疑懼）說什麼？
　　　　（賀伯衝上）

賀　伯：小人只來晚了一步，公主就要搭建「成婚梯」啦。

心　妍：「成婚梯」？

賀　伯：就是納采、問名、納吉、納徵、請期、親迎……那一整
　　　　大套婚禮程序嘛，一階一階踩上去，最後送入洞房啊！

心　妍：啊！這……

莫　愁：（羞）哎呀！（撒嬌，拜下）姐姐！好姐姐！
　　　　（鴿叫聲）

賀　伯：（抬頭看）喲，靳嬤嬤的飛鴿傳書來了，小人去看看。
　　　　（下）

莫　愁：姐姐！

心　妍：唉——
　　　　（旁唱）聲聲嘆、世事難料多意外，
　　　　　　　　陰錯陽差桑作槐。
　　　　　　　　妹妹她、迫不及待結紅綵，
　　　　　　　　少女情竇正初開。
　　　　　　　　嬌俏的鮮花鬢邊戴，
　　　　　　　　傾慕的種子心上栽。

莫　愁：（懇求）姐姐！好姐姐！

心　妍：（接唱）耳邊不住嬌聲喚，
　　　　　　　　怎忍見她淚盈懷？

（嘆氣，白）妹妹啊——

（接唱）婚姻大事非兒戲，

且容為姐——再思再想再安排。

雪　蓮：（介入，向心妍，白）這就對了！「婚姻大事非兒戲」，
　　　　你要牢記啊！

心　妍：是。（旁白）公主莫非在暗示什麼？

莫　愁：（歡喜接唱）同心欲結紅羅帶，

託付姐姐巧剪裁。

（心妍輕拍莫愁）

（賀伯手持小紙條急上）

賀　伯：好消息——大王回宮後，靳嬤嬤已伺機稟報詳情。大王
　　　　查明真相，下令幽禁王后，也已派出禁衛軍迎接二位公
　　　　主。咱們可以收拾行囊，準備回宮了。

心　妍：啊，謝天謝地！

莫　愁：（拍手）太好了，要回宮了！

賀　伯：不過——

心　妍：奶娘還說了什麼？

賀　伯：大王與可汗訂了親……

心妍、莫愁：（大驚）什麼？

賀　伯：靳嬤嬤說為了維持邊境的安寧，大王決定兩國結盟，聯
　　　　姻示好。

心　妍：啊！

（心妍幾乎昏厥，莫愁搶上扶住）

莫　愁：姐姐！這可怎麼辦啊？

心 妍：呀——

   （非常投入，旁唱）實指望、春來紅杏枝頭鬧，

        對鏡梳妝喜眉梢。

        實指望、同心永結花常好，

        情如金石莫逆交。

        又怎知、晴天忽降霹靂雨，

        地動山搖震九霄。

        又怎知、一朝大寒草木槁，

        四野蒼茫舊情拋！

雪 蓮：（旁白）果然不出所料，她心裡只有大王。

心 妍：（接唱）妹妹的心事須調教，

       父王的旨意難勾消。

       驀然裡、五味雜陳、百轉千回、萬般無奈，

       何去何從——身似浮萍漂。

雪 蓮：（介入，向心妍，白）很好，婚慶祝釐就這麼演！最後
   一段尤其關鍵，務必多加留意。

心 妍：（看手稿，驚訝）可是，公主竟然……

雪 蓮：（打斷）正是如此。人生在世，當有主見，勇於追求心
   之所願。假若只能曲意配合，委屈度日，還不如——（指
   手稿）自我了斷。（向心妍，緩慢）你、明白嗎？

心 妍：（心情複雜）是，奴婢明白。

雪 蓮：明白就好。（向眾人）要知道——

   （唱）浮生若夢臺上演，

      形形色色戲中觀。

卑賤鄙陋原形現，

真善美聖日月穿。

寰宇簡約隨幕轉，

優伶評章非一般。

實存具象勝虛幻，

演繹古今成自然。

但能有為勤檢點，

留取惺惺扣心弦。

（白）你們這兩天辛苦些，仔細磨戲，要演得就像真的一樣。

眾　人：公主放心，我等一定盡力。

雪　蓮：（指手稿，向梅團長）這一段再重排一遍，那公主應該……

（雪蓮、梅團長低聲討論）

心　妍：（自言自語）我所演的是公主的人生，那我自己的人生呢？

莫　愁：你在想什麼？

心　妍：哦，我在想——公主的人生若真能改寫，那咱們的是不是也都可以呢？

賀　伯：當然！（對觀眾）這會兒不就已經改了嗎？

（切光）

第六場　忘情

（鄔酉國王宮，大殿）

（音樂起，眾侍衛、眾宮女、眾大臣、緋櫻、姬總管上，各就定位）

【幕後伴唱】：翠華葳蕤自生光，

　　　　　　珍珠璀璨露凝香。

　　　　　　玉京嬝嬛百花放，

　　　　　　碧瓦紅欄不尋常。

　　　　　　鐵馬多情簷前唱，

　　　　　　金猊歡娛夜未央。

（梅團長衝上，拉住姬總管）

梅團長：大人，大人……

姬總管：什麼事？這麼慌慌張張的？

梅團長：飾演優哈的賀伯，昨日在後臺被布景絆倒，跌下樓梯，摔斷了腿……

姬總管：（怒極）梅團長，你捅出這麼大的婁子，現在這戲要怎麼演？

【畫外音】大王駕到！公主駕到！

姬總管：你呀你……自己不要腦袋便罷了，還不知要怎麼連累老夫！

梅團長：大人放心，小的已連夜拜託辛團長來頂這個小花臉……

（鄔酉王、雪蓮上）

姬總管：哼，算你乖覺！滾！

梅團長：小人告退。（下）

（鄔酉王、雪蓮就位）

【幕後接唱】：君王恩寵錫封賞，

　　　　　　　百年好合鳳求凰。

姬總管：啟稟大王，這梅劇團……呃，和辛劇團聯手演出……

　　　　　（看戲單，詫異）《錯——中——錯》，恭祝婚慶！

鄔酉王：好！

姬總管：開演！

（臺上表演區燈亮，梅團長上）

梅團長：《錯中錯》前情提要，讓鑼鼓告訴您——（下）

　　　　　（鑼鼓經一段。心妍飾桔梗著男裝改扮甄即事，與天珩飾谷連天上，二人小圓場對看）

天　珩：賢弟急急催我前來，莫非有要事相商？

心　妍：兄長，實不相瞞，小弟——便是桔梗。

天　珩：啊！你是桔梗公主？

心　妍：正是。

天　珩：（再三打量，驚喜）賢弟——不，公主，你瞞得愚兄好苦！

心　妍：兄長啊——

　　　　　（唱）並非我有心來隱瞞，

　　　　　　　　須防東海波浪翻。

　　　　　　　　父王回宮是非斷，

　　　　　　終究撥雲見青天。

天　玽：（接唱）我為公主長吁嘆，

　　　　　　　　　家門不幸百慮煎。

　　　　　　　　　幸有賢弟時相伴，

　　　　　　　　　山林生活亦安然。

　　　　　　　　　賢弟你、頃刻之間身分換，

　　　　　　　　　離愁依依柳含煙。

心　妍：兄長誤會了——

　　　　（接唱）辭別兄長入京去，

　　　　　　　　　請旨賜婚不日還。

天　玽：（大喜，接唱）春風得意楊柳岸，

　　　　　　　　　　　蜂蝶先後採花鮮。

　　　　　　　　　　　形影相依不嫌晚，

　　　　　　　　　　　否極泰來谷連天。

心　妍：（接唱）舍妹對你另眼看，

　　　　　　　　　喜結佳藕並蒂蓮。

天　玽：（大驚）什麼？令妹——鈴蘭公主？

心　妍：正是。鈴蘭對兄長一往情深，若結連理，必能琴瑟和鳴，

　　　　幸福圓滿。

天　玽：這、這是從何說起……那、那——你呢？

心　妍：兄長啊——

　　　　（接唱）小妹奉旨入契丹，

　　　　　　　　　兩國締盟天下安。

　　　　　　　　　奈何曲終人將散，

　　　　　　兄長恩情記心間。

　　　　　　徒嘆此生因緣淺，

　　　　　　來世重修共嬋娟。

天　珩：不、不——

　　　　（接唱）聞此言、霎時間、天昏地暗，

　　　　　　寸心宛如萬箭穿。

　　　　　　曾經滄海難為水，

　　　　　　神傷不覺遍體寒。

　　　　　　敢辭厚愛雀屏選，

　　　　　　深情無語問蒼天。

心　妍：兄長何須如此？

天　珩：不！今生今世，惟卿一人！

　　　　（接唱）此生果然福分淺，

　　　　　　　我決意、遁空門、檻外再修來世緣。（決絕下）

心　妍：兄長……（拭淚）

雪　蓮：情有所鍾，唯心是問。大王說對嗎？

鄔酉王：這……

　　　　（唱）情有所鍾唯伊人，

　　　　　　今後卻要兩離分。

　　　　　　欲捨難捨捫心問，

　　　　　　船過豈能水無痕？

　　　　（辛團長飾優哈上）

辛團長：公主，您這是何苦呢？

心　妍：傻子，你不懂。

·可　待·

辛團長：這有什麼難懂？谷公子對您情深意重，您卻偏要把他和
　　　　鈴蘭公主湊成一對兒。娶一個不愛自己的人，或嫁一個
　　　　自己不愛的人，哎喲，說有多苦就有多苦啊！
　　　　（心妍泣，雪蓮亦泣）
鄔酉王：（動容，旁唱）意中人兒半掩面，
　　　　　　　　　　　　梨花帶雨亦堪憐。
　　　　（向心妍，接唱）莫不是新聲搬演違心願？
　　　　（向雪蓮，接唱）莫不是鄉關萬里夢魂牽？
　　　　　　　　　　　　莫不是連日歡宴身乏倦？
　　　　（沉吟，接唱）莫不是──另有隱情口難言？
雪　蓮：（向鄔酉王，接唱）此中別有真誠意，
　　　　　　　　　　　　但請大王靜心觀。
鄔酉王：（疑惑，旁白）難道這戲有什麼弦外之音？
心　妍：（唱）天生萬物依其序，
　　　　　　　　花開花謝自有時。
雪　蓮：（起身，接唱）日月運行太初始，
　　　　（鄔酉王驚，眾臣亦驚）
心　妍：（接唱）陰陽無私名兩儀。
雪　蓮：（接唱）何人主宰定機制？
心　妍：（接唱）物化尊卑分高低。
雪蓮、心妍：（接合唱）主體豈能任交易？
　　　　　　　　　　　定靜籌謀宜省思。
心　妍：（悲痛欲絕）不，我不能──
　　　　（唱）眼看他歡歡喜喜花堂拜，

·50·

　　　　　　卻只能自家心事心底埋。

　　　　　　若要我聯姻遠去千里外，

　　　　　　倒不如就此翻開生死牌！

　　　　　（拔劍自刎，假戲真做）

雪　蓮：（奪劍）且慢！

鄔酉王：（衝上抱住心妍）哎呀──心妍！

姬總管：哎呀！糟了！

眾　臣：（大驚，紛紛阻攔）大王不可！這是演戲啊！

鄔酉王：（向心妍）你沒有受傷吧？

　　　　（環視周圍，尷尬）孤王失態了！（放開心妍）

　　　　（正色，向姬總管）這就是總管保證的愛情喜劇嗎？

姬總管：（惶恐）大王，微臣保證的是……《好彩頭》，不知怎

　　　　麼變成了《錯中錯》。這可是……（趕快卸責）公主欽

　　　　點的戲啊。

鄔酉王：（不解）這是怎麼回事？

雪　蓮：啟稟大王，確實是雪蓮修改了原作──

　　　　（唱）聯姻豈能名利換？

　　　　　　　成事在人不在天。

　　　　　　　兩情相悅朝夕伴，

　　　　　　　日久自然繫良緣。

　　　　（上前牽起心妍）

心　妍：（再次入戲，接唱）海誓山盟難盤算，

　　　　　　　　　　　心誠不過踐前言。

　　　　　　　　　　　假戲真作情難辨，

離合悲歡若等閒。

雪　蓮：（接唱）于歸鄔酉非所願，

心　妍：（接唱）無能自主空自憐。

雪　蓮：（接唱）夢裡徜徉千山遠，

心　妍：（接唱）世外何處有桃源？

　　　　（眾皆詫異）

鄔酉王：（嚴肅）你們究竟何意？

雪　蓮：大王，王兄遣嫁，雪蓮不得不應命而行。然而……

鄔酉王：然而如何？

雪　蓮：大王厚愛，雪蓮感激不盡。只是，因緣不計名利，恩情並非愛情。兩國聯姻不容自主，有違人道，還望大王明察。

鄔酉王：但聯姻足以維繫兩國邦誼，綿延子嗣，永保太平啊。

雪　蓮：維繫兩國邦誼，當以誠信為上。互助合作，禮尚往來。何必勉強活生生的人呢？若要雪蓮強顏歡笑，這般人生豈非太過無趣？尚且不如劇中人了。

姬總管：大王聖明。女子無知無識，只要三從四德，乖乖聽話就好。絕對不要讓她們說話，也不要聽她們說話，以免自找麻煩。

鄔酉王：（喝斥姬）多口！

　　　　（向雪蓮）那——依公主之見？

雪　蓮：大王啊——

　　　　（唱）世事未能一概論，

　　　　　　　人情也有百樣新。

> 行如傀儡終天恨，
>
> 惟求自由抵萬金。
>
> 戲中演戲說根本，
>
> 解鈴還須繫鈴人。

鄔酉王：（沉吟）這……

姬總管：大王，兩國聯姻自古而然，從未聽聞公主自悔婚約這等奇事！

眾　臣：（議論紛紛）是啊、是啊！不能悔婚！破壞邦交，後果不堪設想！

雪　蓮：大王，兩國聯姻，若非情願，結果何曾圓滿？雪蓮萬不得已，出此下策。尚請大王三思。

姬總管：此事傳揚出去，豈非鄔酉一大醜聞？大王萬萬不可俯允。

雪　蓮：此事傳揚出去，天下更感大德。大王恩寬，必有後福。

（上前牽起心妍）何況心妍姑娘對大王一片赤忱——

（向鄔酉王，唱）豈不聞在世易得千金寶，

　　　　　一生難遇有情人。

　　　　　您與她靈犀互通性相近，

　　　　　應羨鴛鴦不羨仙。

姬總管：（向觀眾）老夫就知道，一旦讓女人多說兩句話，可就要天下大亂了。

眾　臣：（大驚，喧騰擾攘）萬萬不可、萬萬不可！貴賤有別，這可不亂了倫理？萬萬不可！

鄔酉王：唉——

（旁唱）雖則是倫理自古有定制，

代代相傳萬世基。

雖則是兩國締約佳話始，

萬邦來朝齊祝釐。

公主她婉拒絲蘿言成理，

善自為謀條縷析。

可嘆孤詞窮一時難盡意，

如何兩全費心機。

（深思狀）

（看雪蓮）不忍她、身在鄔西心存異，

（看心妍）不忍她、獨上高樓眼迷離。

（看雪蓮）不忍她、悒悒寡歡難如意，

（看心妍）不忍她、夜闌人靜常淒淒。

（稍停，續唱）這廂是千斤重擔家國事，

那廂是念念不忘夢中思。

（稍停，續唱）雄才大略竟無計，

去留之間兩游移。

一念容或開先例，

猶恐他日嗟何及……

姬總管：大王，這心妍姑娘只是個優伶，身分卑微，實在不適合……

眾　臣：為了和平，兩國一定要聯姻，這婚慶大典也要繼續進行啊！

鄔西王：這……

雪　蓮：大王，既然聯姻勢在必行，那也罷了——就請容本宮先

行攜帶心妍回國。

鄔酉王：什麼？公主你……？

　　　　（眾臣大驚）

雪　蓮：本宮有意認下心妍作為義妹，奏請王兄冊封公主。大王
　　　　啊——

　　　　（唱）貴賤由天不由己，

　　　　　　　際遇原有得與失。

　　　　　　　容留片刻悲轉喜，

　　　　　　　莫待他年悔恨時。

　　　　　　　秦晉和諧依住例，

　　　　　　　花開來春亦未遲。

　　　　　　　相期可待重逢日，

　　　　　　　笑談勸進杯酒時。

鄔酉王：啊！公主的意思是——？

雪　蓮：來年請大王親自迎娶紫嫛的心妍公主吧！

鄔酉王：（感動）公主，請受本王一拜！

心　妍：（亦下拜）多謝公主！

雪　蓮：從此這兩國之間——

鄔酉王：我鄔酉與紫嫛，世世代代永為兄弟之邦！

眾　臣：恭喜！恭喜！恭喜大王！恭喜心妍姑娘！

　　　　（眾人定格）

　　　　（切光）

尾　聲

（字幕：半年後）

【畫外音】：大王起駕！

　　　　（鄔酉王車隊緩緩行進）

【幕後伴唱】：秋去春來萬象始，

　　　　　　　往訪故人問舊題。

　　　　　　　世界猶如一舞臺，

　　　　　　　上場下場各有時。

　　　　　　　聚散縱然緣情起，

　　　　　　　悲喜也要半存疑。

　　　　　　　成就關目惟彼此，

　　　　　　　山高水長或可期，或可期。

劇　終

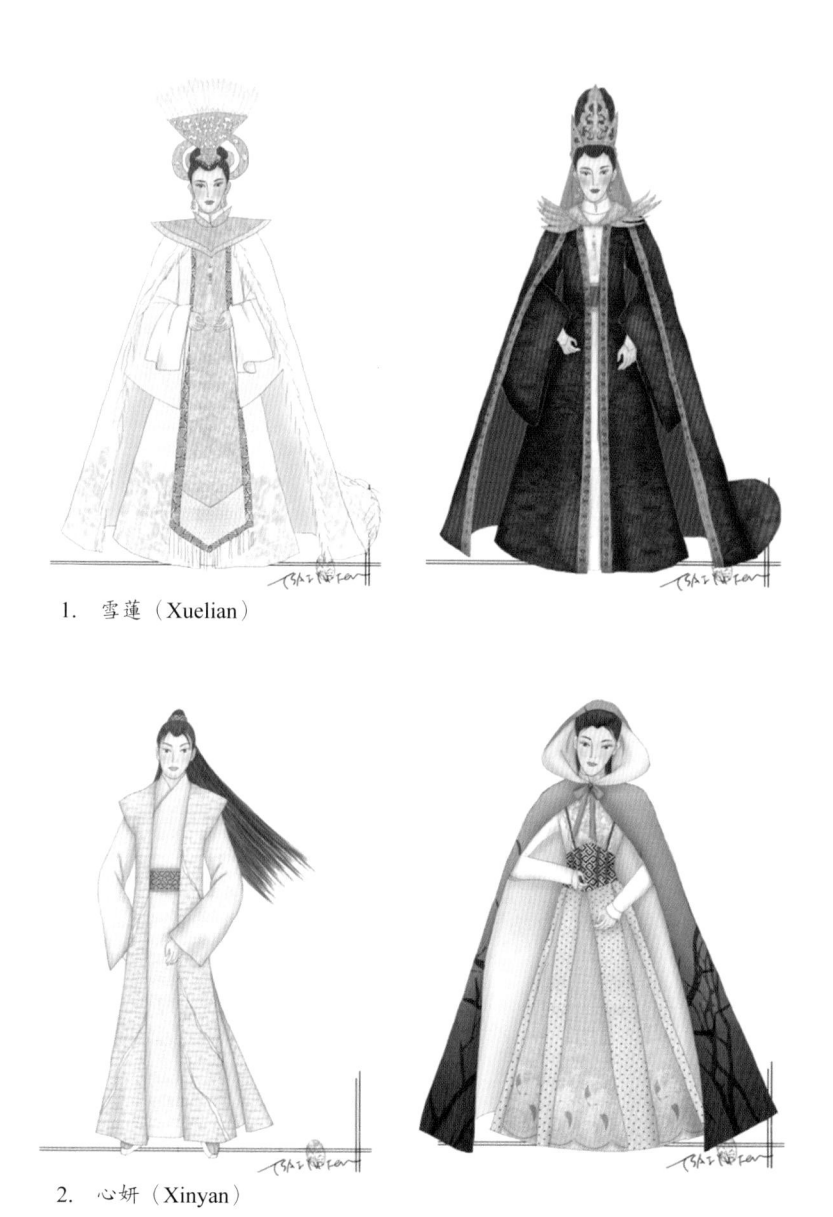

1. 雪蓮（Xuelian）

2. 心妍（Xinyan）

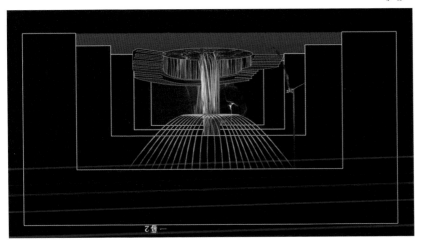

第一幕

幕之2

3. 國王（The King）

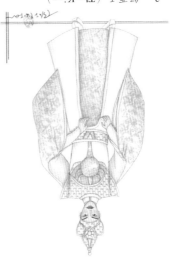

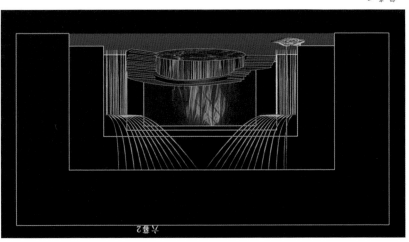

六輯2

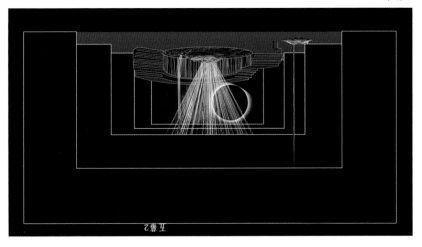

五輯2